BENNY AND PENNY

IN

THE TOY BREAKER

GEOFFREY HAYES

BENNY AND PENNY *IN* THE TOY BREAKER

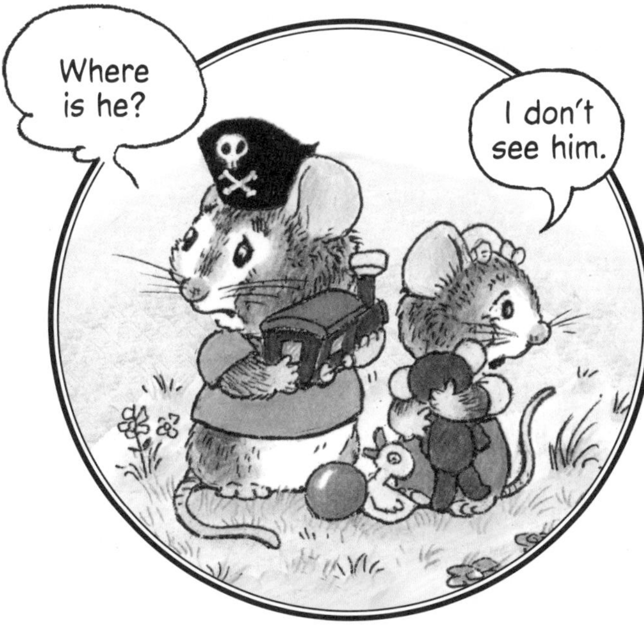
Where is he?
I don't see him.

A TOON BOOK BY

GEOFFREY HAYES

TOON BOOKS is a division of RAW Junior, LLC, New York

For Leigh Stein,

who is Penny in disguise

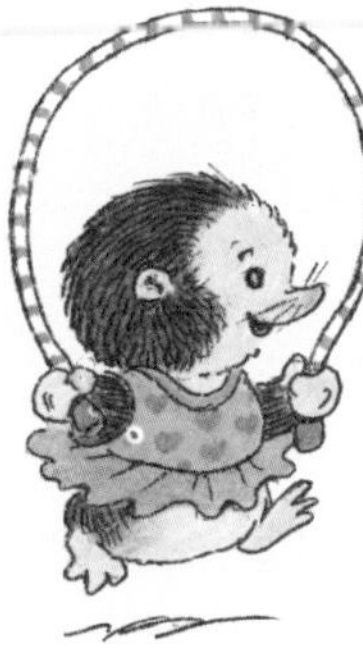

Editorial Director: FRANÇOISE MOULY
Advisor: ART SPIEGELMAN

Book Design: FRANÇOISE MOULY & JONATHAN BENNETT

A TOON BOOK

Library of Congress Cataloging-in-Publication Data:
Hayes, Geoffrey.
Benny and Penny and the toy breaker : a Toon Book / by Geoffrey Hayes.
p. cm.
Summary: When their cousin Bo comes to visit, Benny and Penny hide their toys and try to go on a treasure hunt without him, but Bo will not stop pestering them.
ISBN 978-1-935179-07-8
1. Graphic novels. [1. Graphic novels. 2. Bullies–Fiction. 3. Brothers and sisters–Fiction. 4. Cousins–Fiction. 5. Mice–Fiction.] I. Title. II. Title: Toy breaker.
PZ7.7.H39Bdm 2010
[E]–dc22

2009038066
ISBN 13: 978-1-935179-07-8 ISBN 10: 1-935179-07-1
10 9 8 7 6 5 4 3 2 1

WWW.TOON-BOOKS.COM

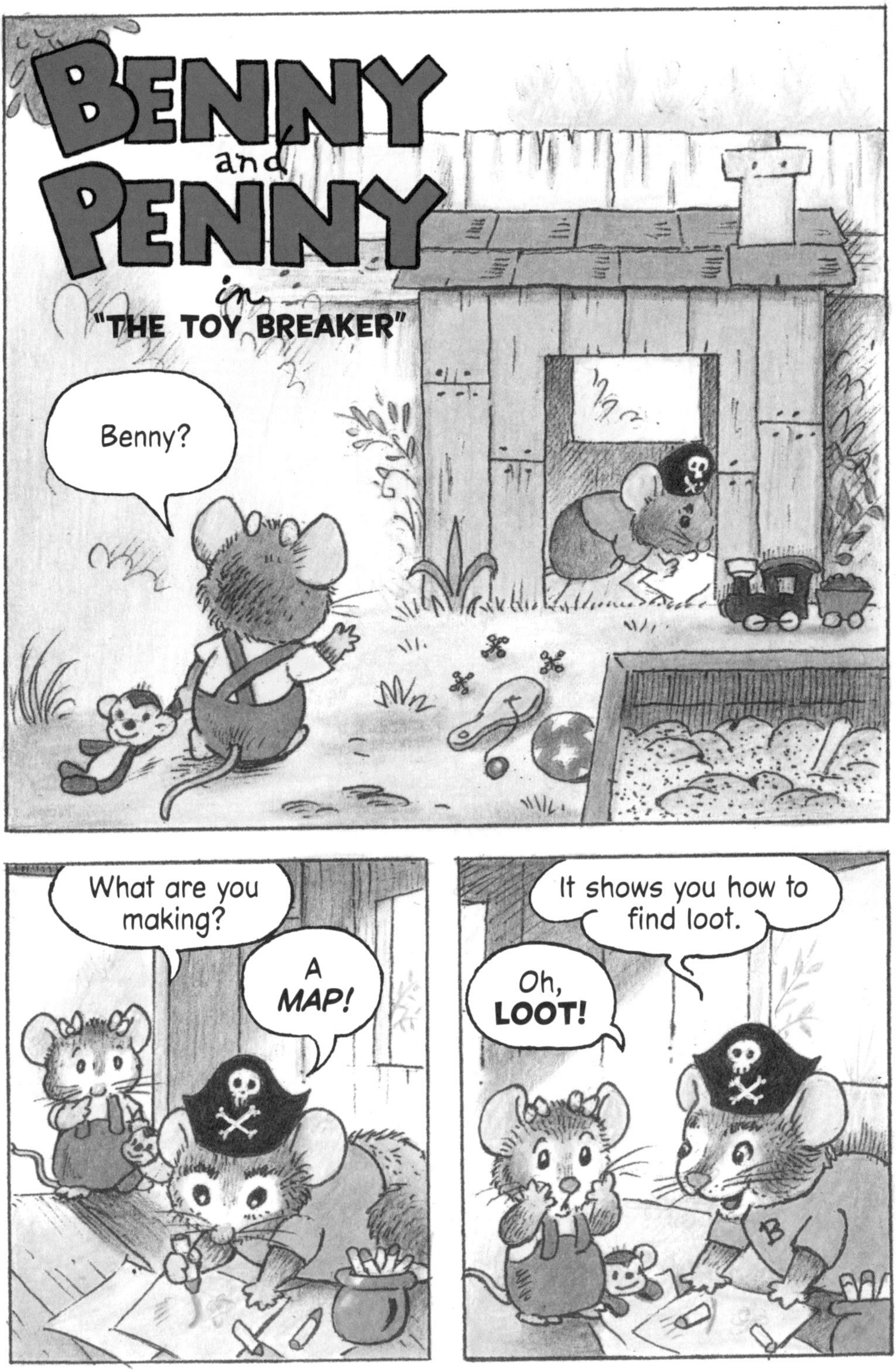
BENNY and PENNY
in "THE TOY BREAKER"
Benny?
What are you making?
A MAP!
It shows you how to find loot.
Oh, LOOT!

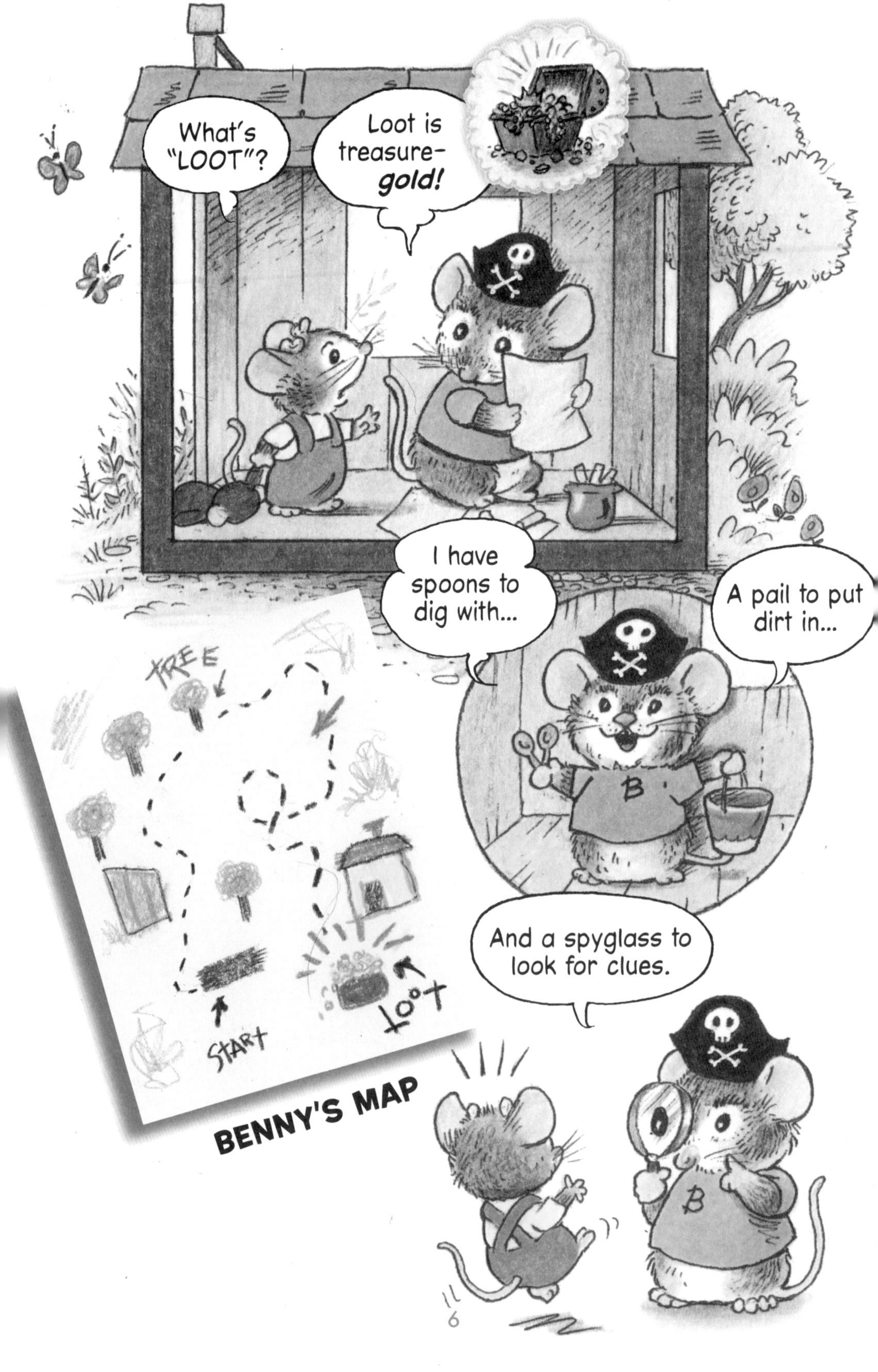
What's "LOOT"?
Loot is treasure-gold!
I have spoons to dig with...
A pail to put dirt in...
And a spyglass to look for clues.
TREE
START
LOOT
BENNY'S MAP

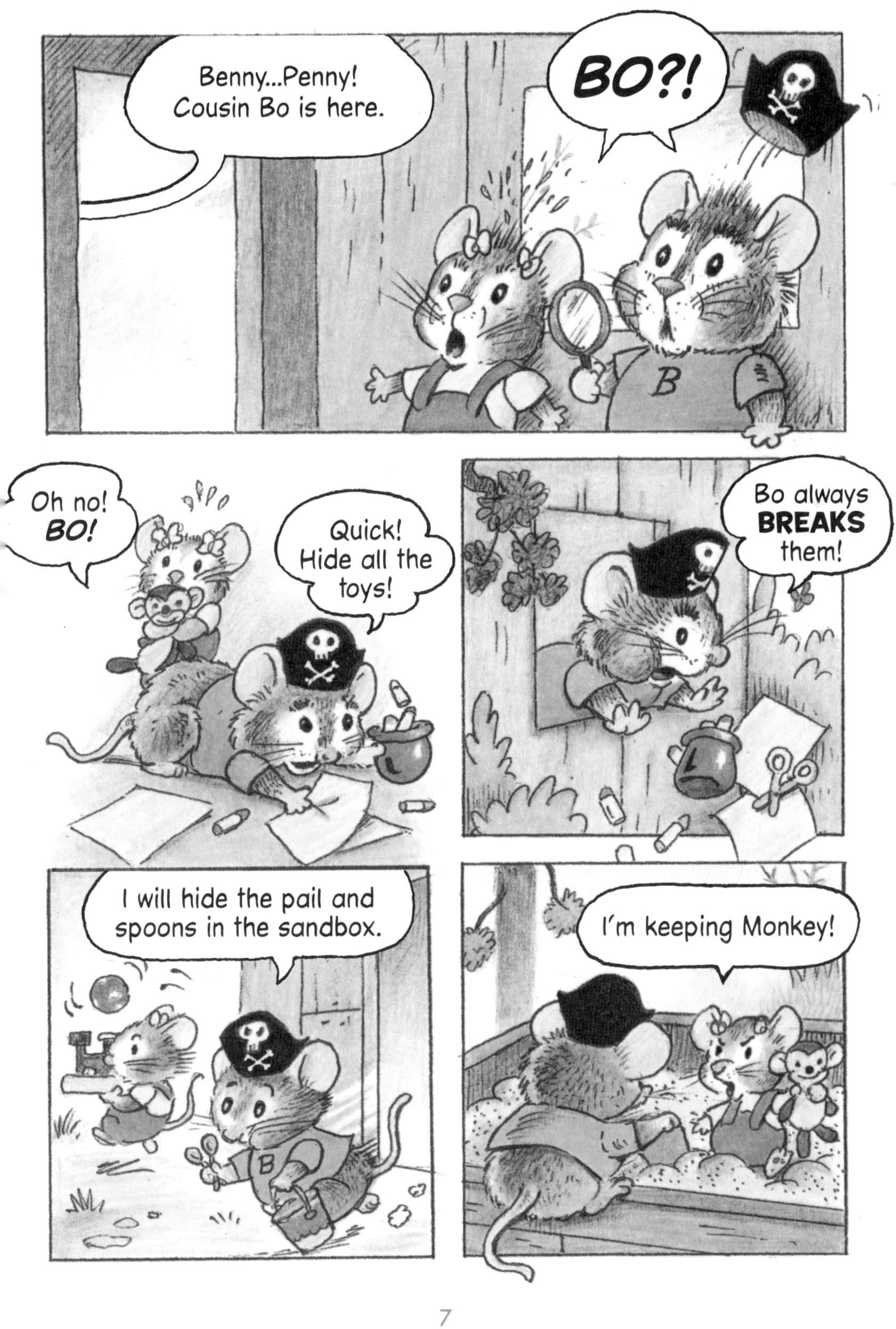
Benny...Penny!
Cousin Bo is here.
BO?!
Oh no!
BO!
Quick!
Hide all the
toys!
Bo always
BREAKS
them!
I will hide the pail and
spoons in the sandbox.
I'm keeping Monkey!

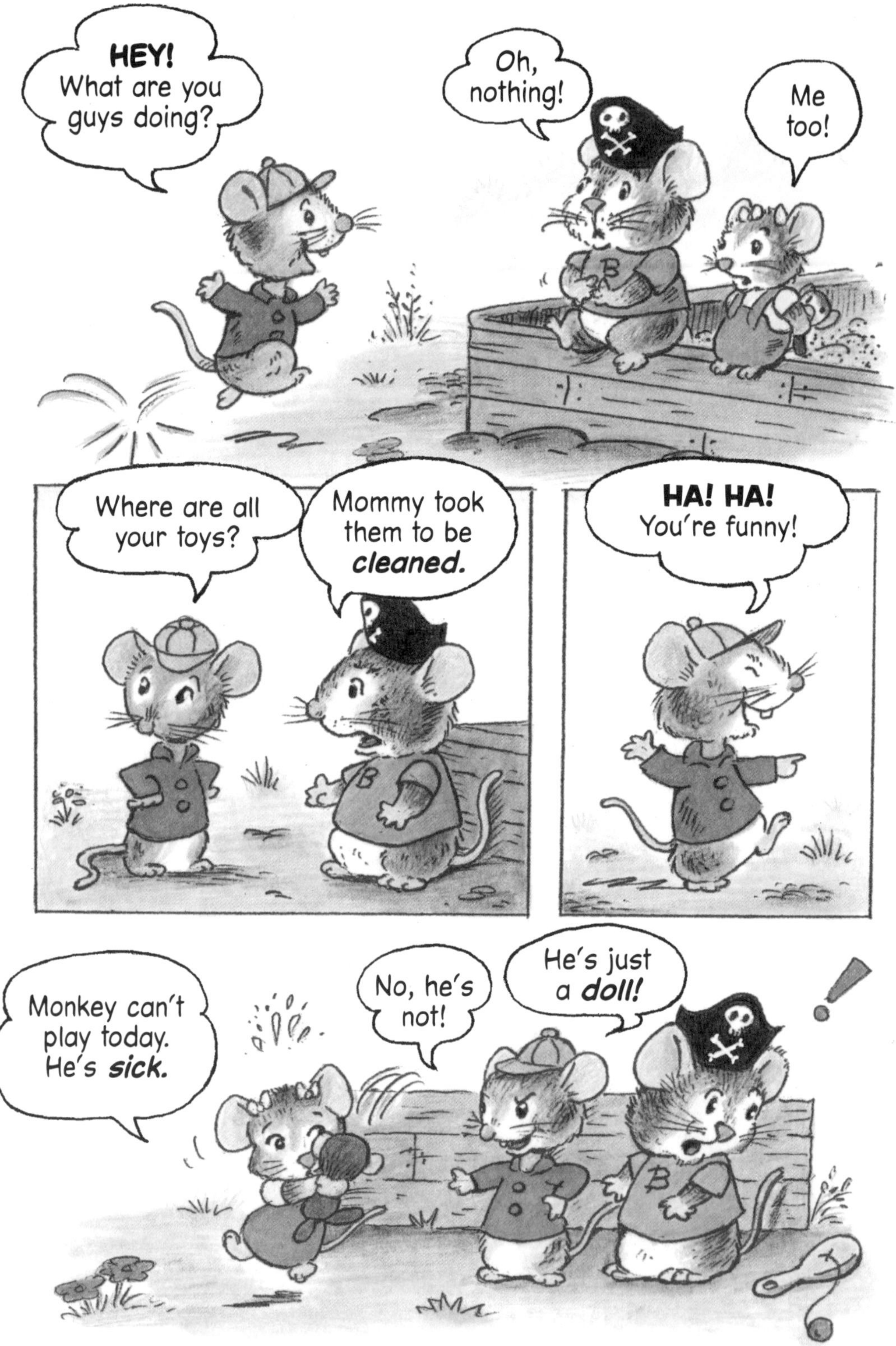
HEY! What are you guys doing?
Oh, nothing!
Me too!
Where are all your toys?
Mommy took them to be ***cleaned.***
HA! HA! You're funny!
Monkey can't play today. He's ***sick.***
No, he's not!
He's just a ***doll!***

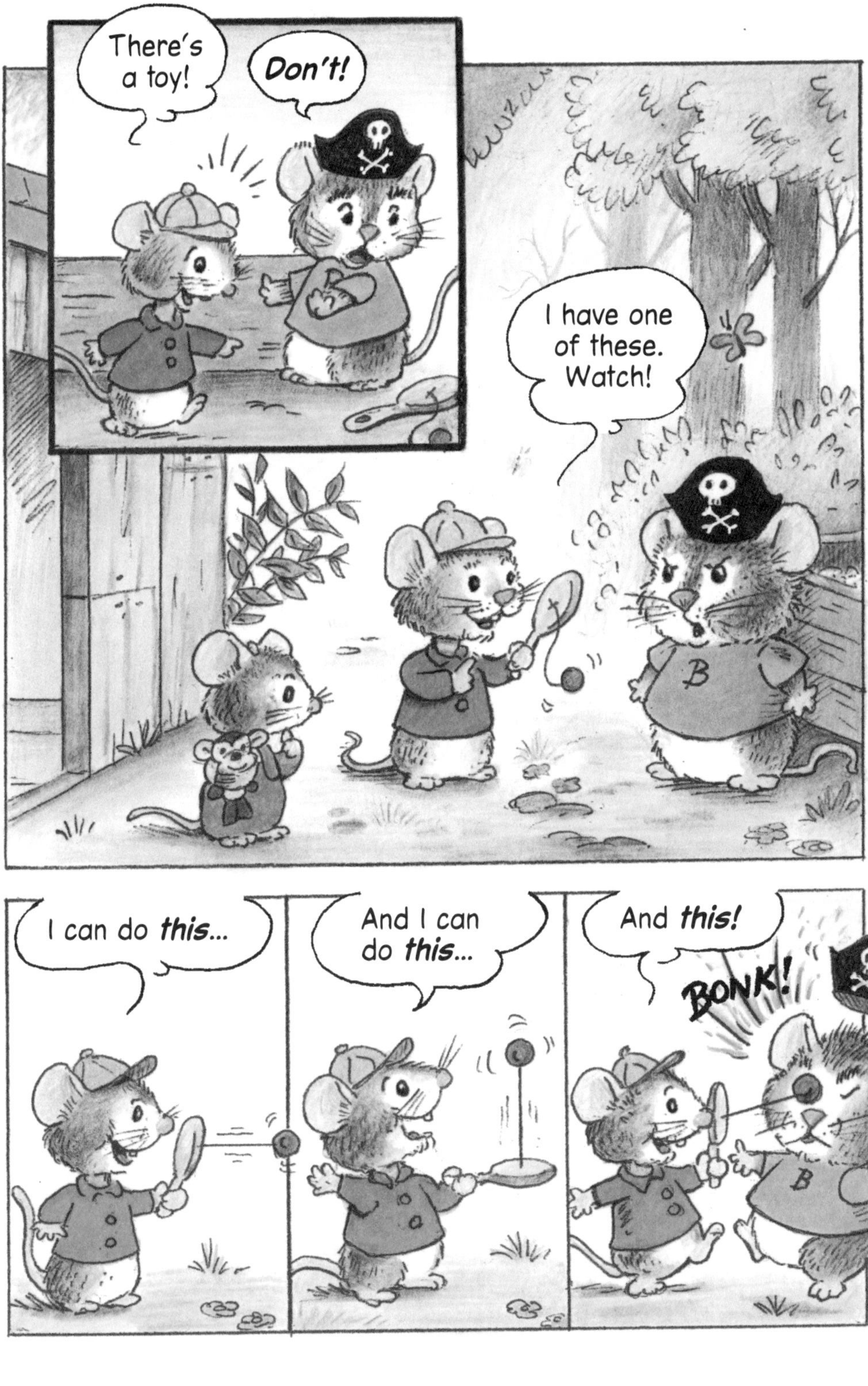
There's a toy!
Don't!
I have one of these. Watch!
I can do this...
And I can do this...
And this!
BONK!

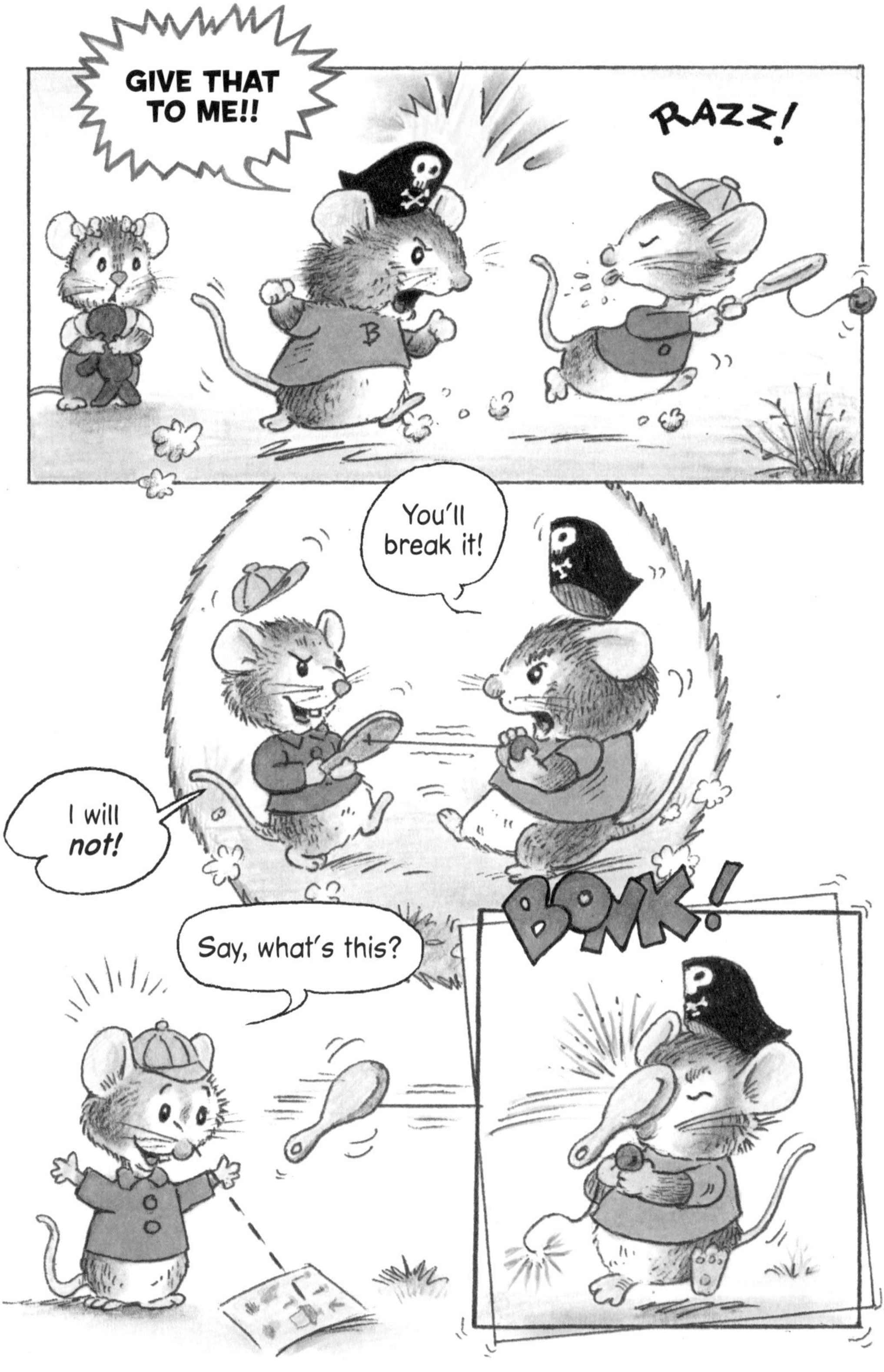
GIVE THAT TO ME!!
RAZZ!
You'll break it!
I will *not!*
Say, what's this?
BONK!

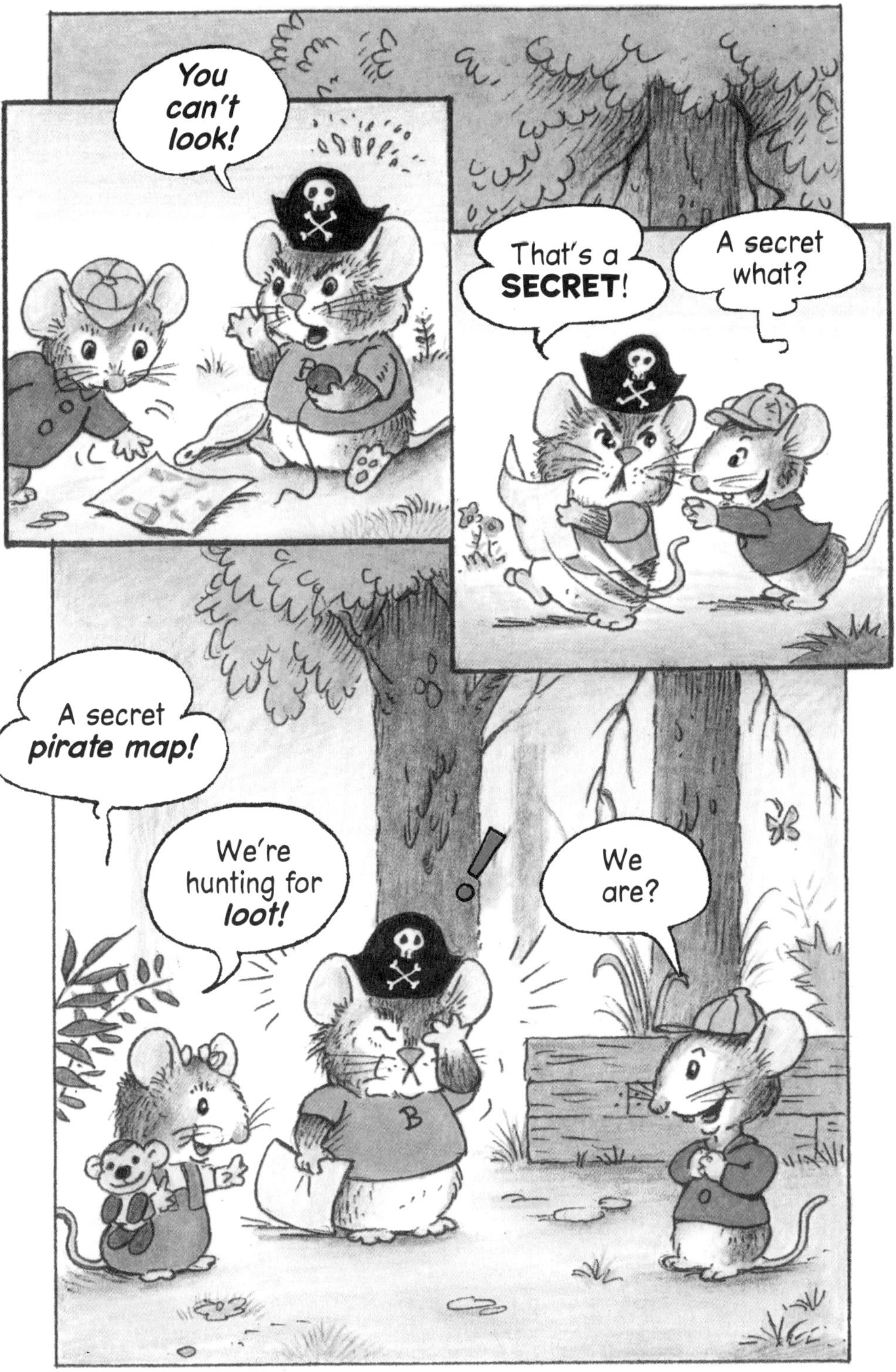
You can't look!
That's a **SECRET**!
A secret what?
A secret *pirate map!*
We're hunting for *loot!*
!
We are?

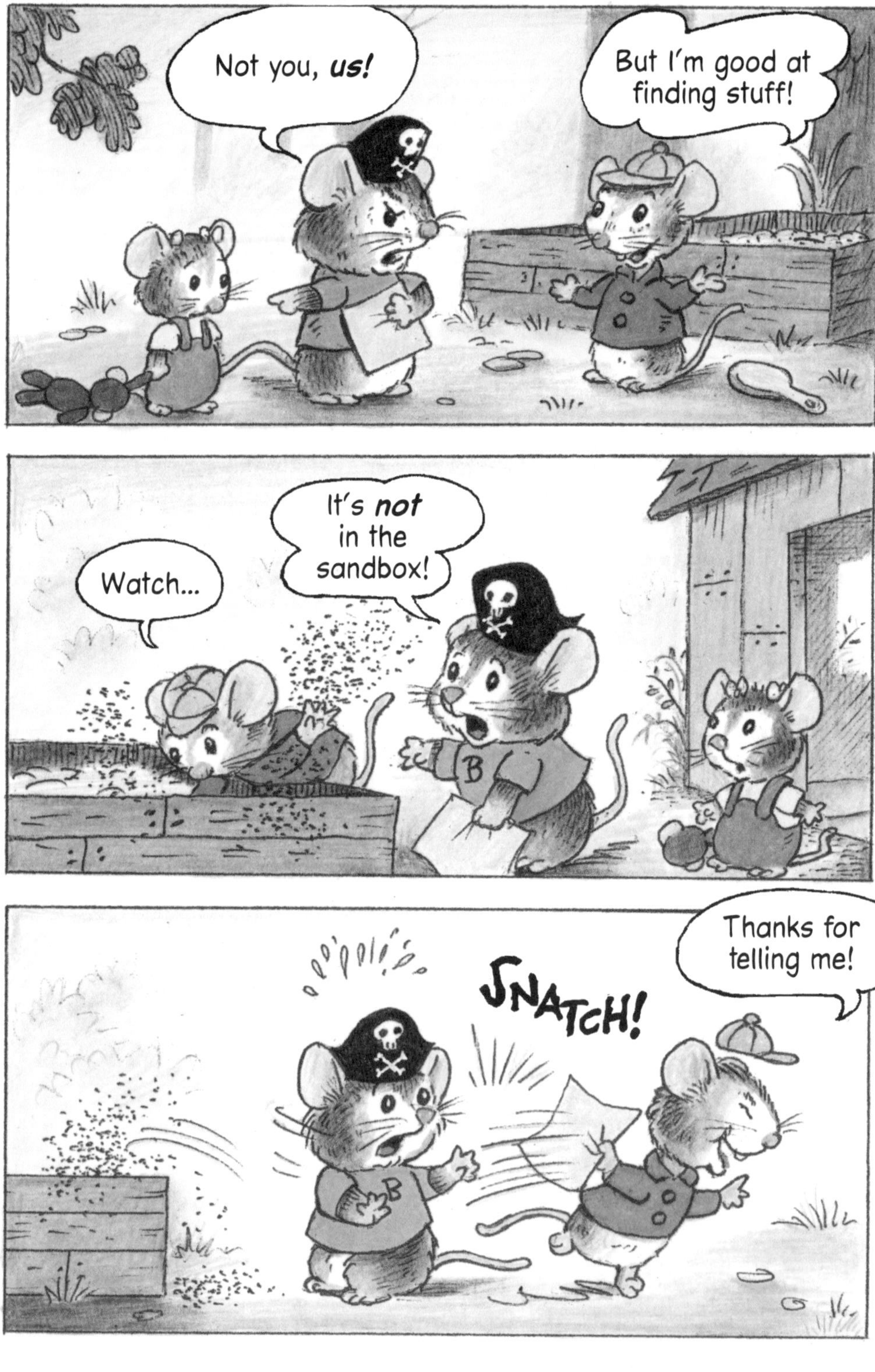
Not you, ***us!***
But I'm good at finding stuff!
Watch...
It's ***not*** in the sandbox!
SNATCH!
Thanks for telling me!

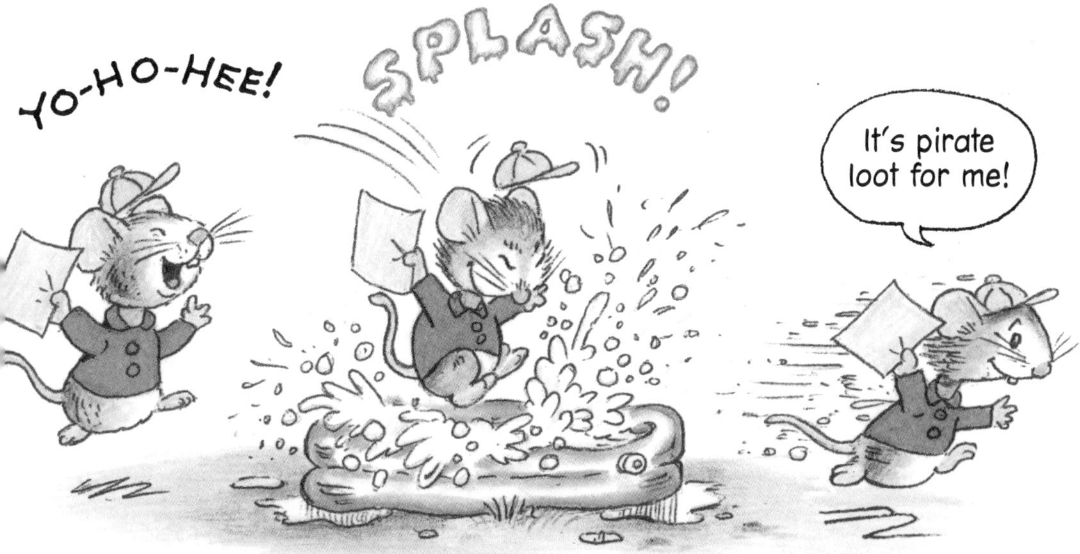
YO-HO-HEE!
SPLASH!
It's pirate loot for me!

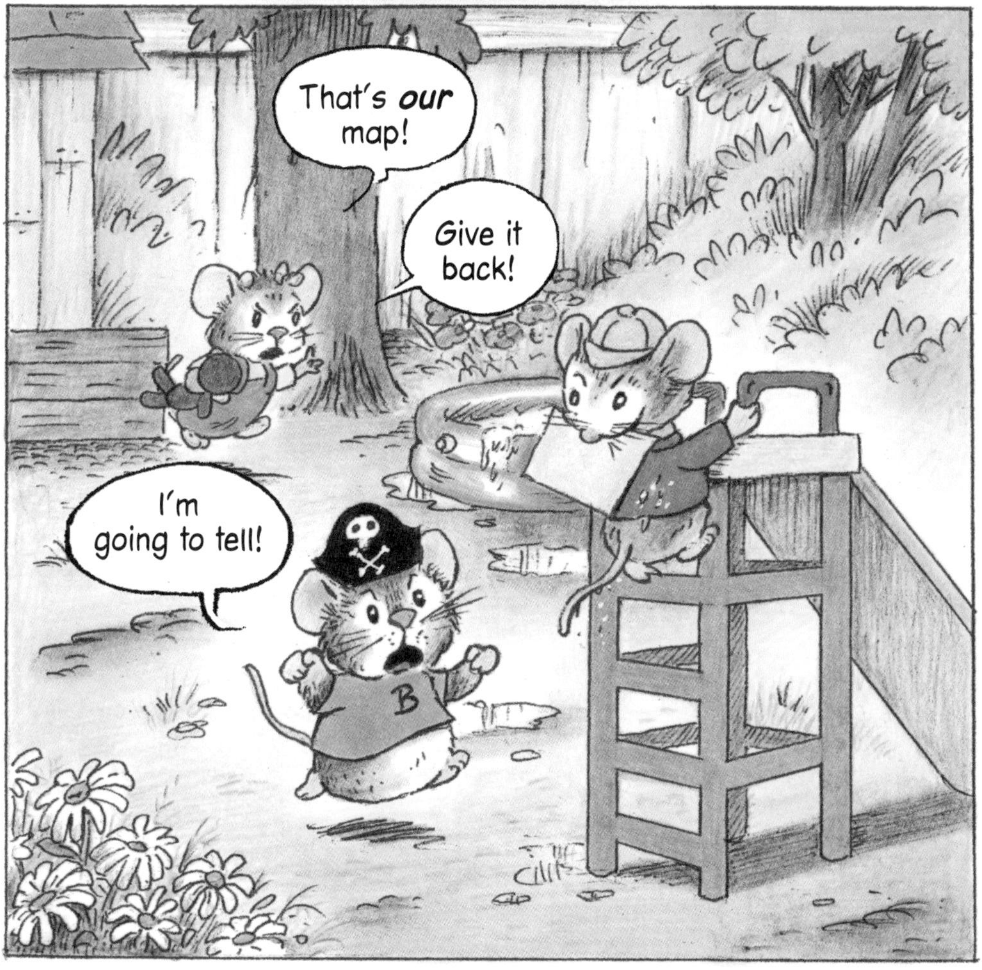
That's *our* map!
Give it back!
I'm going to tell!

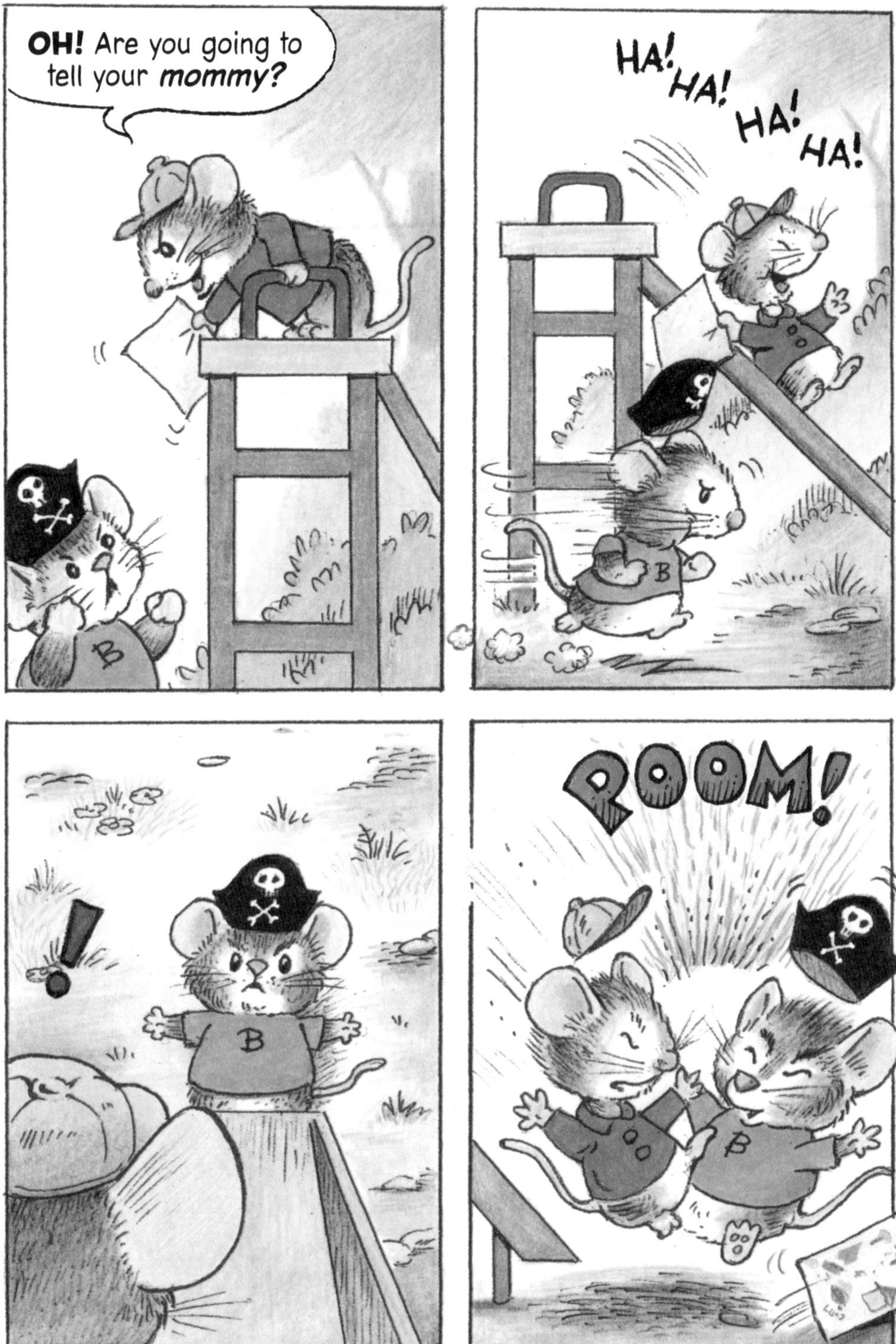
OH! Are you going to tell your *mommy?*
HA! HA! HA! HA!
!
ROOM!

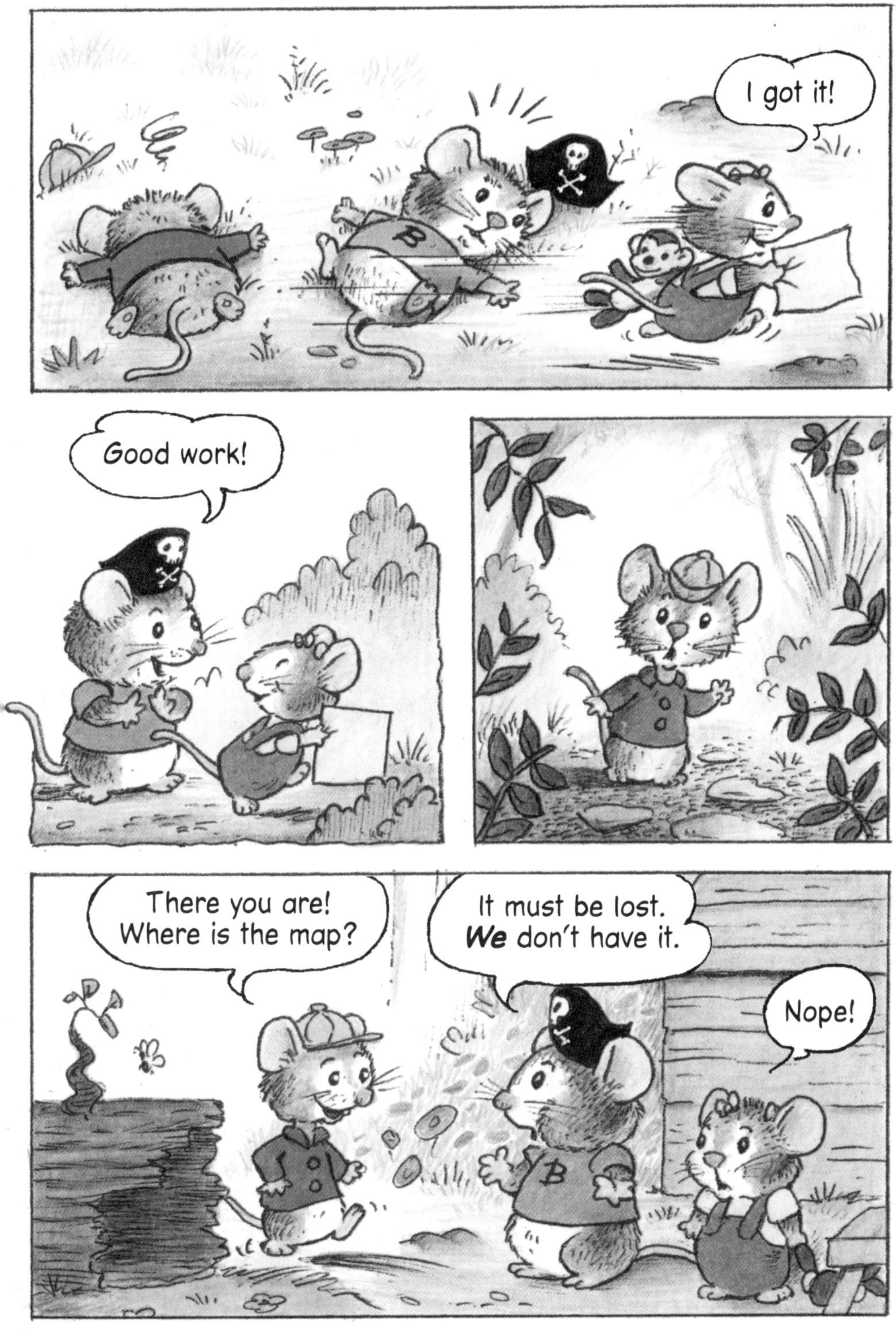
I got it!
Good work!
There you are! Where is the map?
It must be lost. *We* don't have it.
Nope!

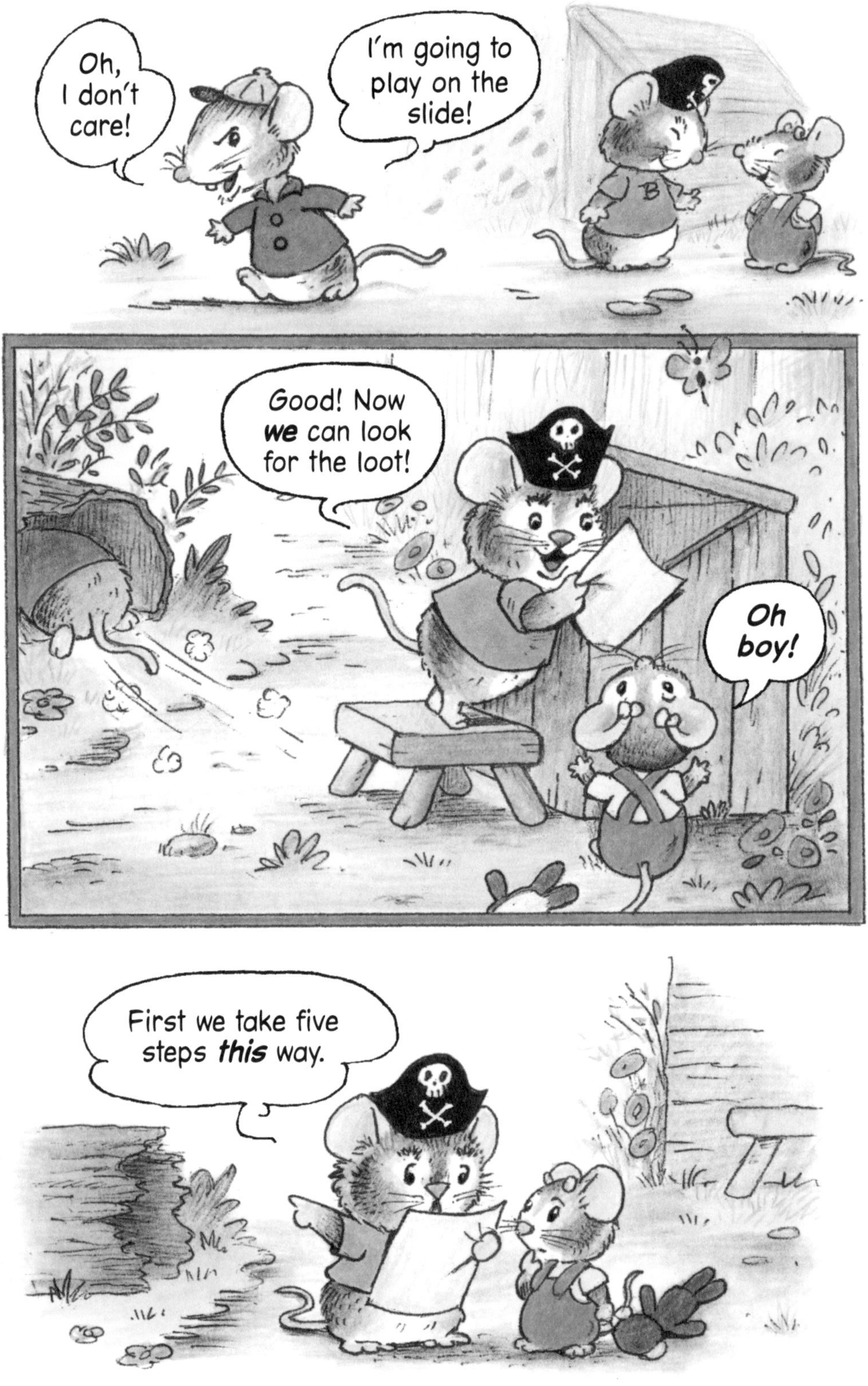
Oh, I don't care!
I'm going to play on the slide!
Good! Now ***we*** can look for the loot!
Oh boy!
First we take five steps ***this*** way.

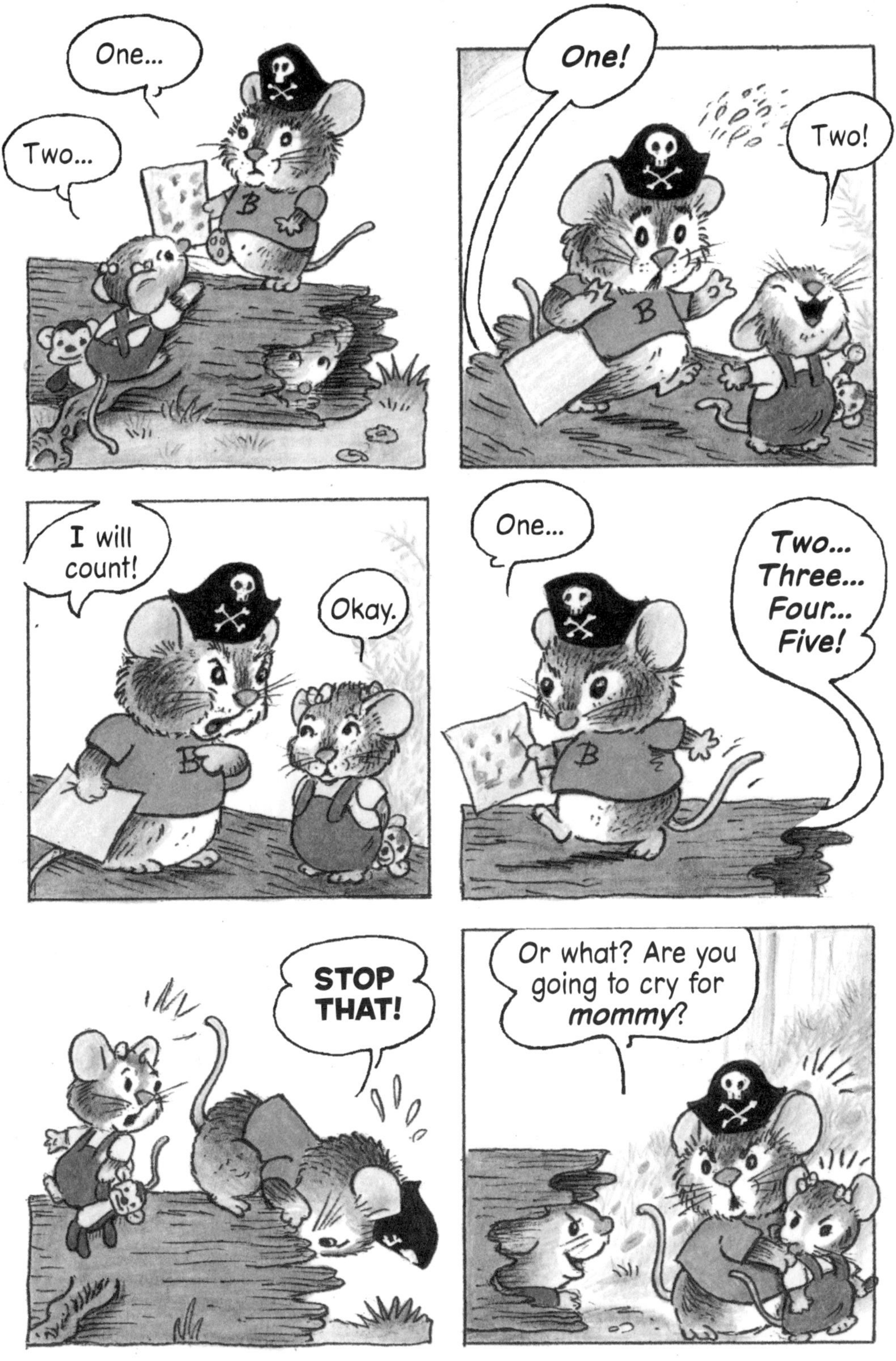
One...
Two...
One!
Two!
I will count!
Okay.
One...
Two... Three... Four... Five!
STOP THAT!
Or what? Are you going to cry for *mommy*?

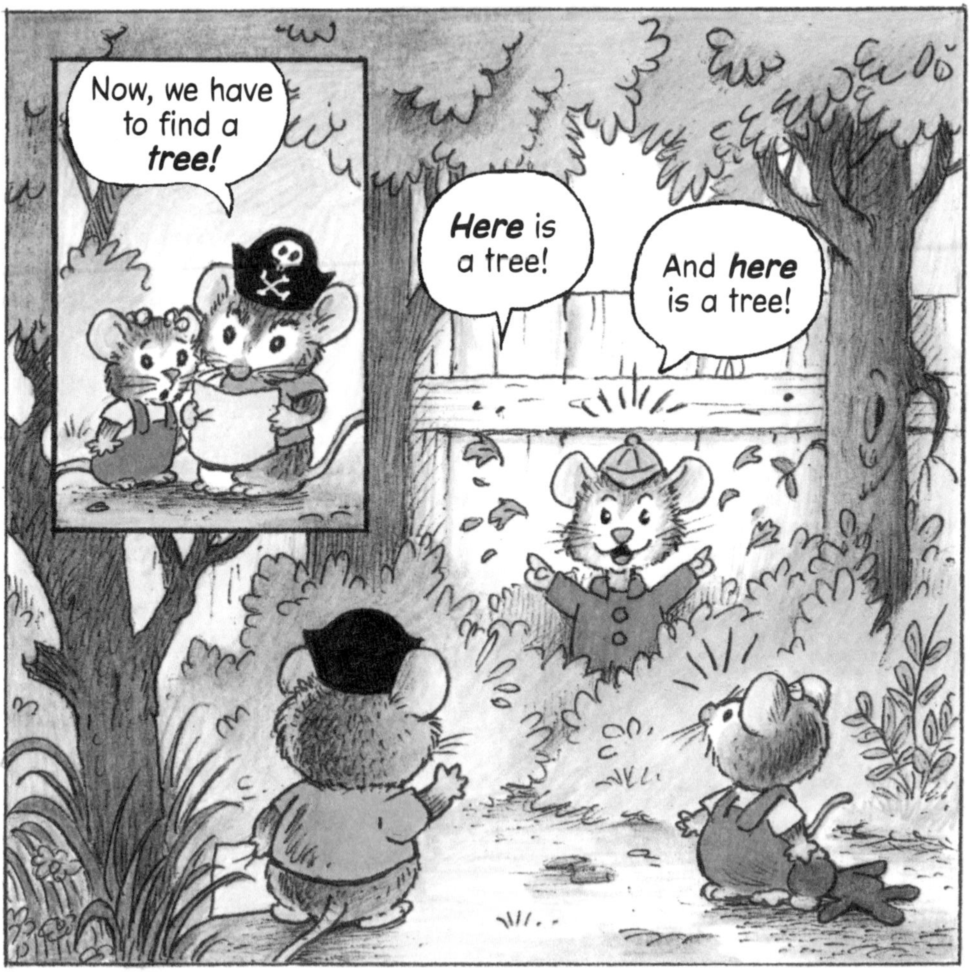
Now, we have to find a *tree!*
Here is a tree!
And *here* is a tree!

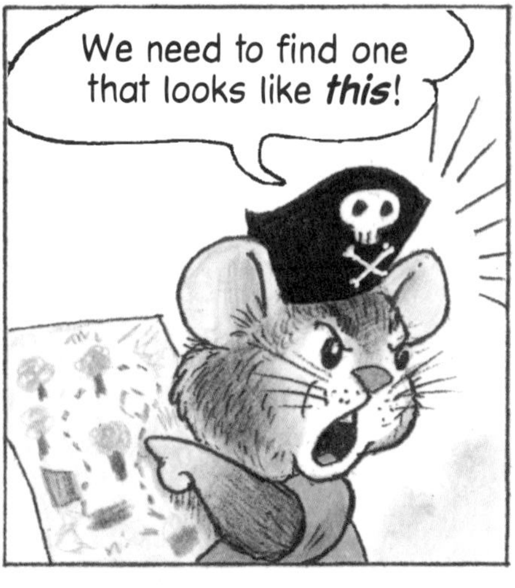
We need to find one that looks like *this*!

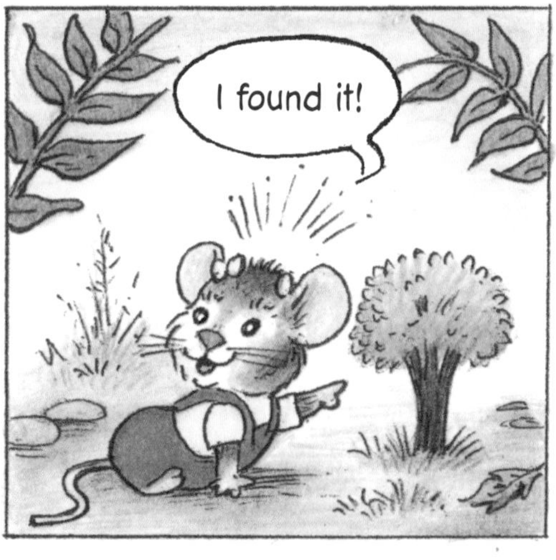
I found it!

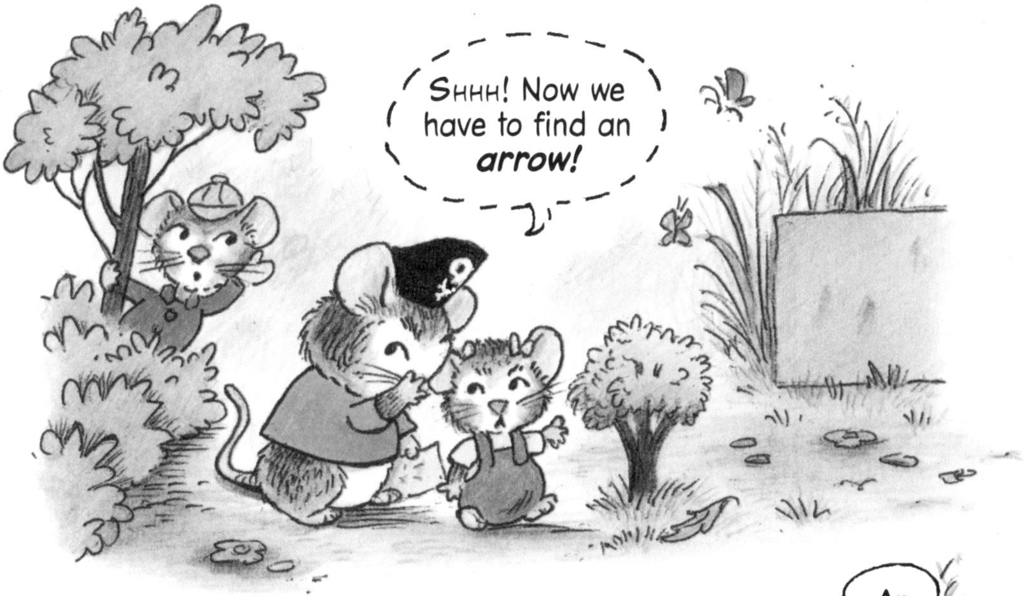
SHHH! Now we have to find an *arrow!*

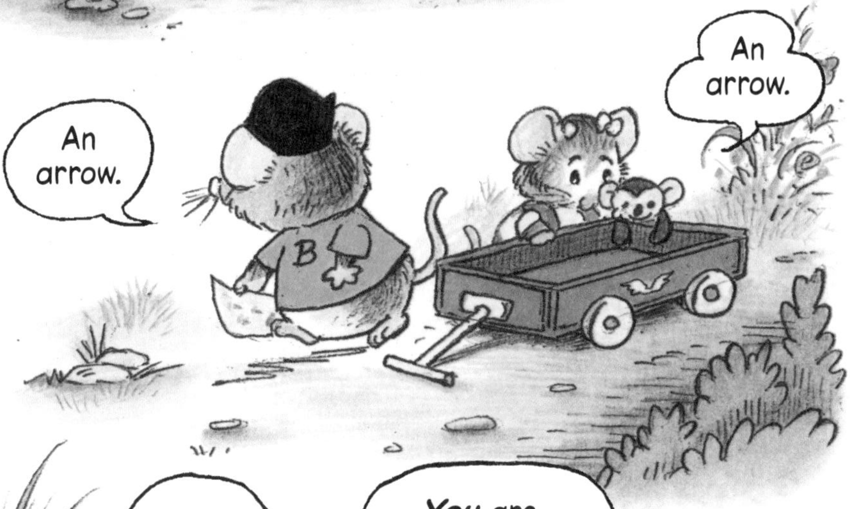
An arrow.
An arrow.

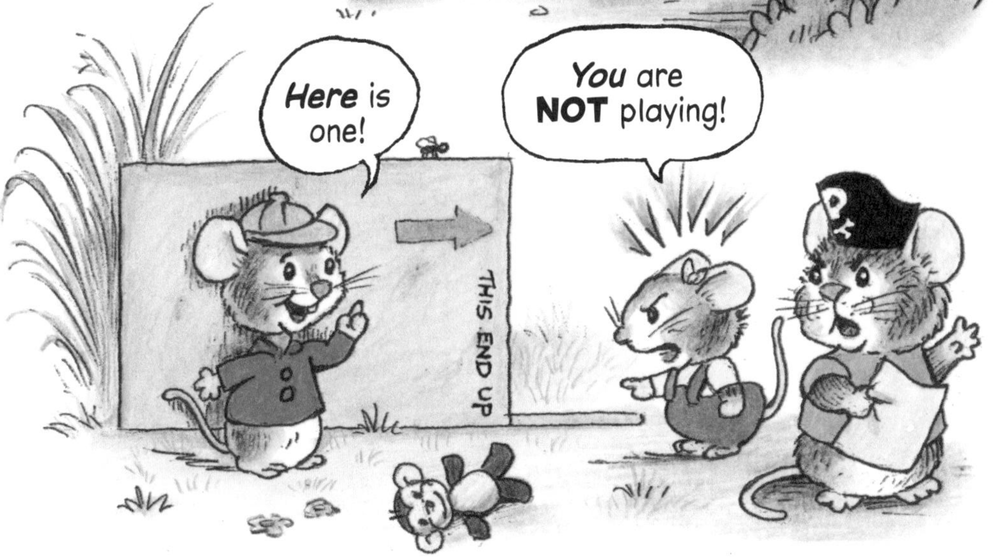
Here is one!
You are **NOT** playing!
THIS END UP

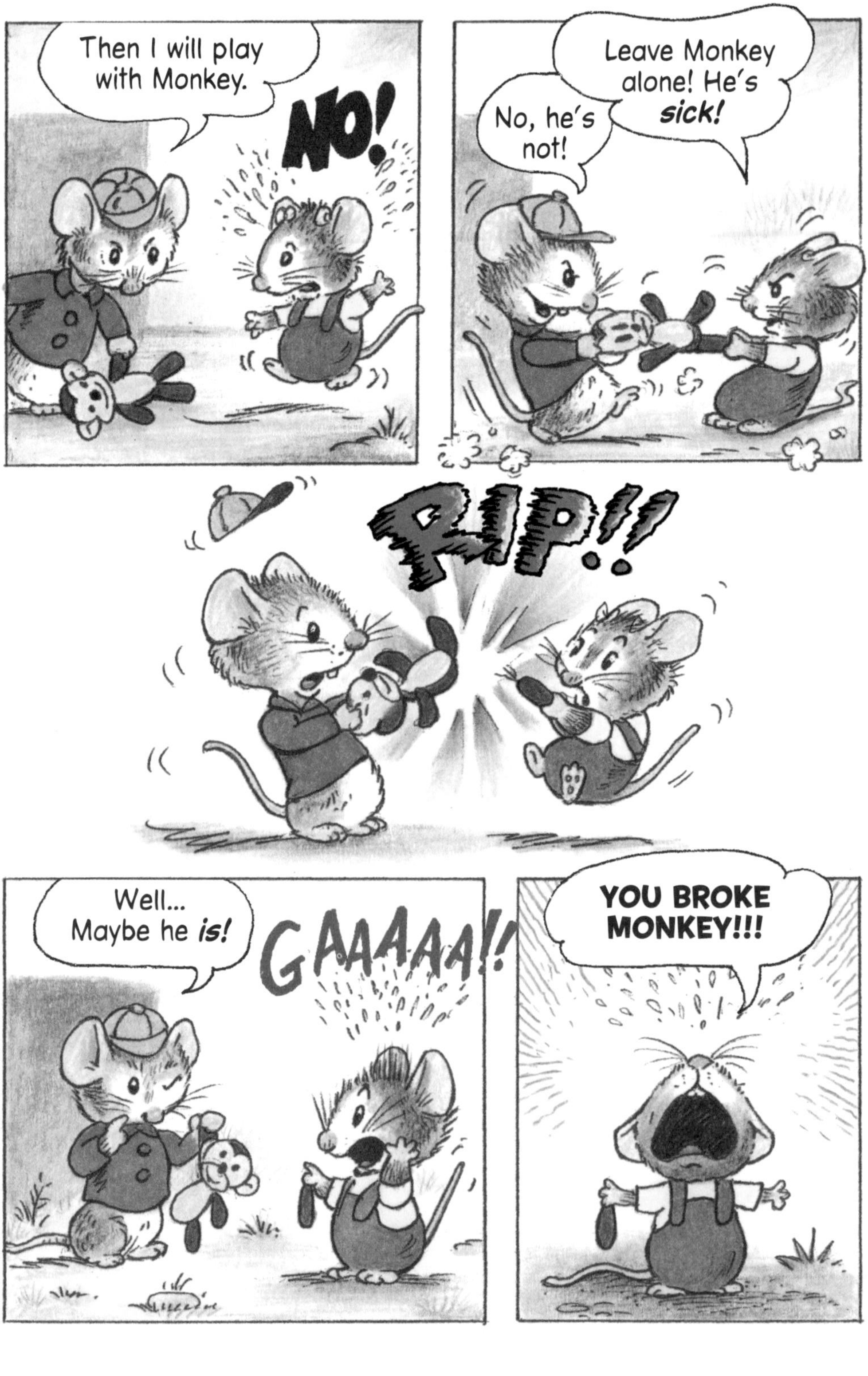
Then I will play with Monkey.
NO!
Leave Monkey alone! He's *sick!*
No, he's not!
RIP!!
Well... Maybe he *is!*
GAAAAA!!
YOU BROKE MONKEY!!!

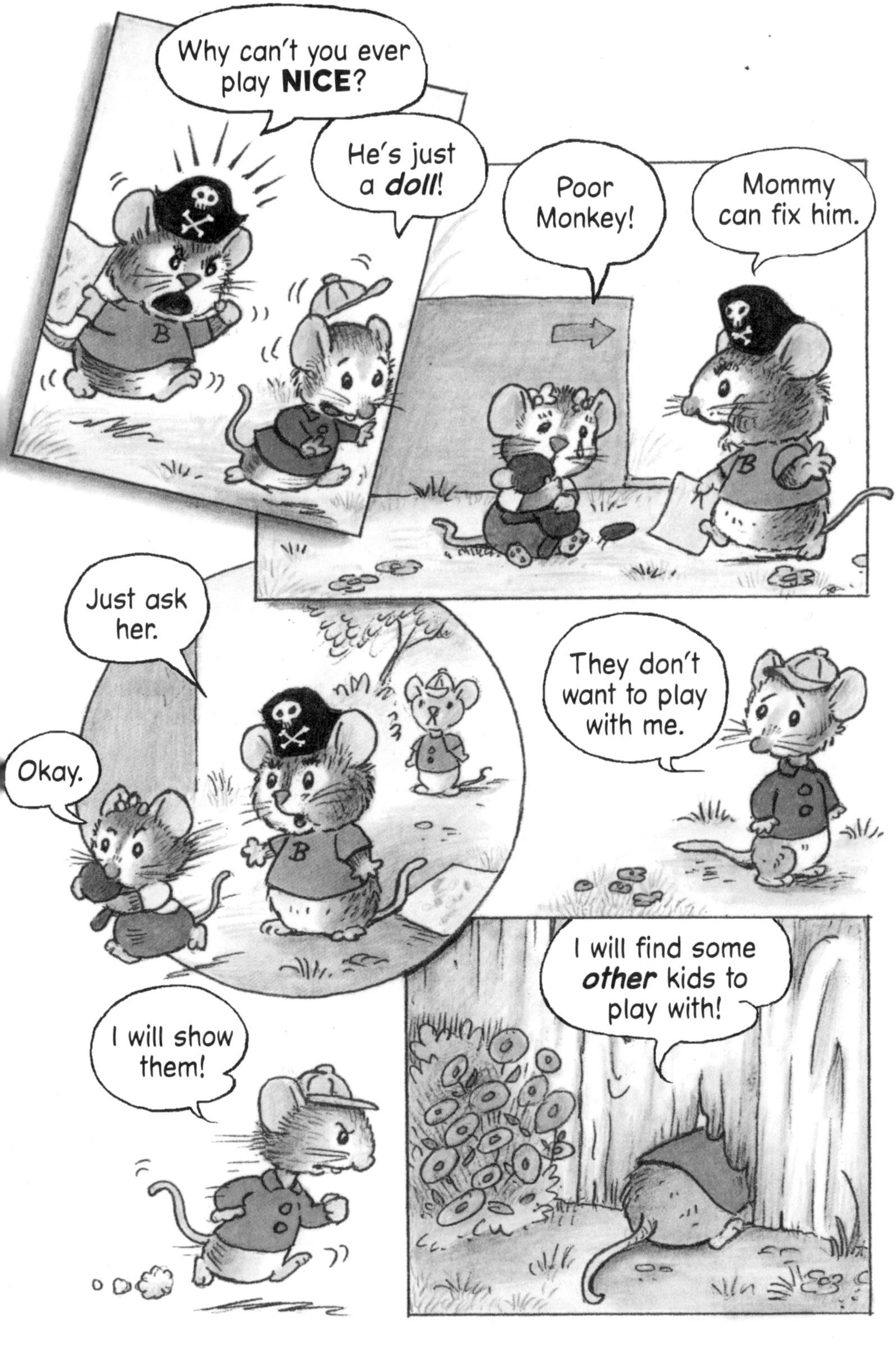
Why can't you ever play **NICE**?
He's just a ***doll***!
Poor Monkey!
Mommy can fix him.
Just ask her.
Okay.
They don't want to play with me.
I will show them!
I will find some ***other*** kids to play with!

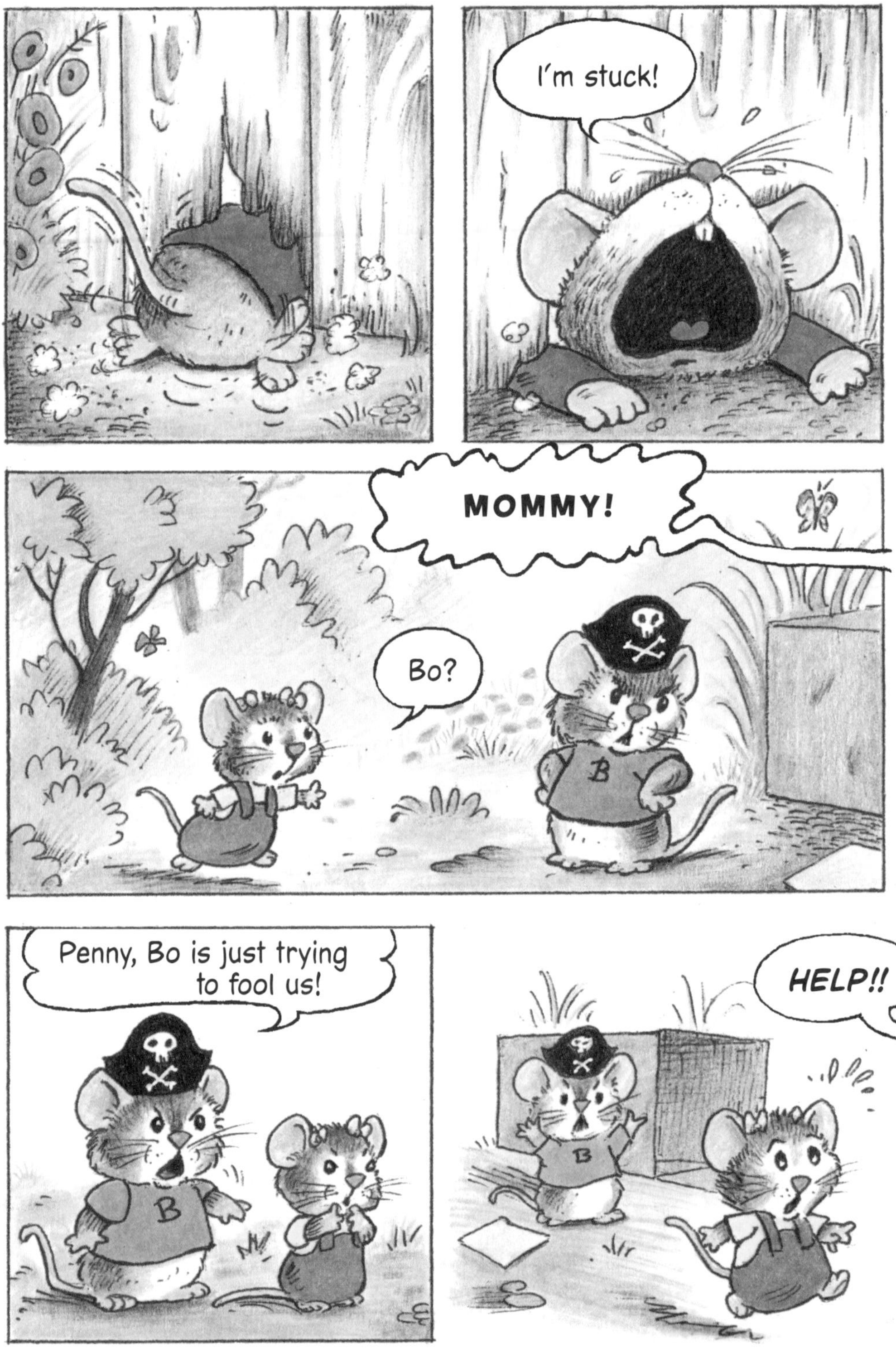
I'm stuck!
MOMMY!
Bo?
Penny, Bo is just trying to fool us!
HELP!!

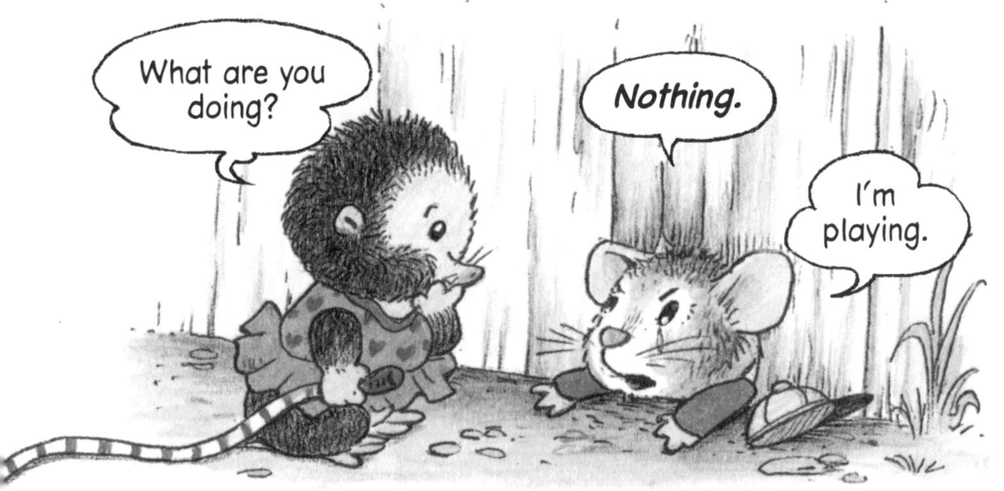
What are you doing?
Nothing.
I'm playing.

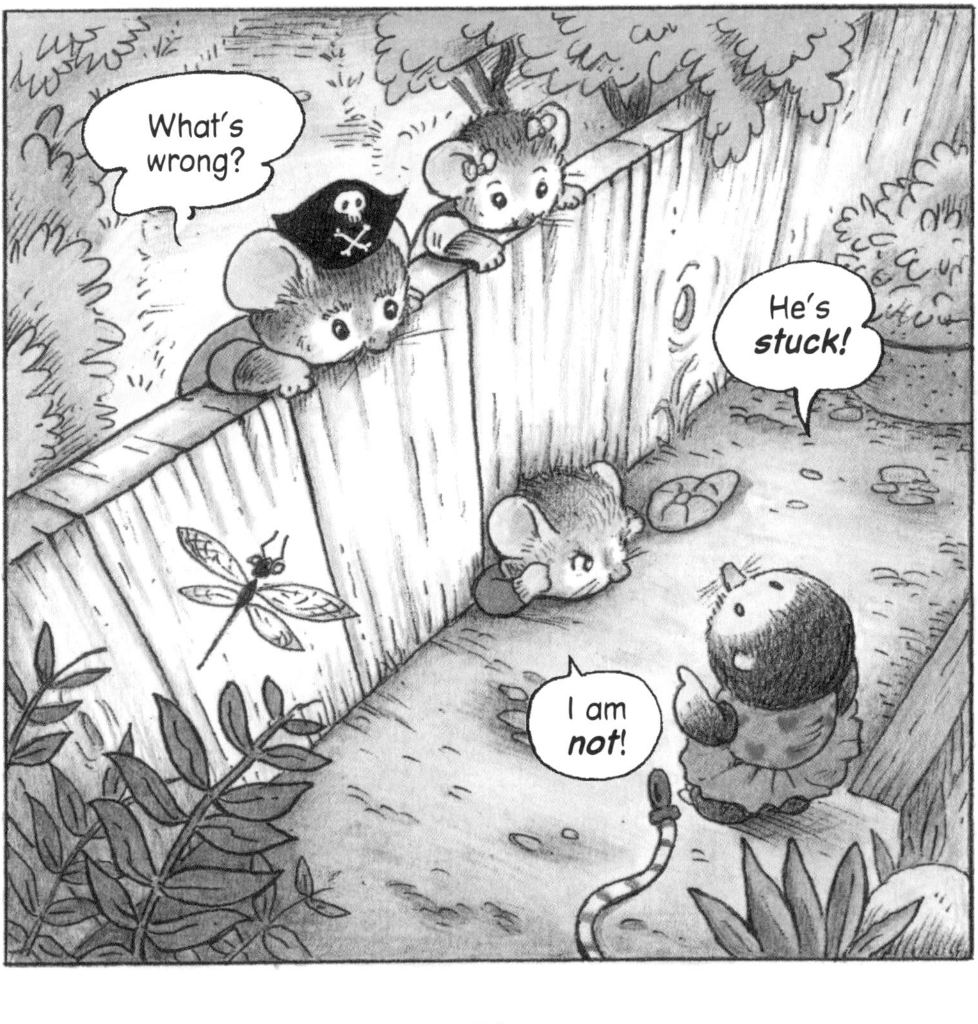
What's wrong?
He's ***stuck!***
I am ***not***!

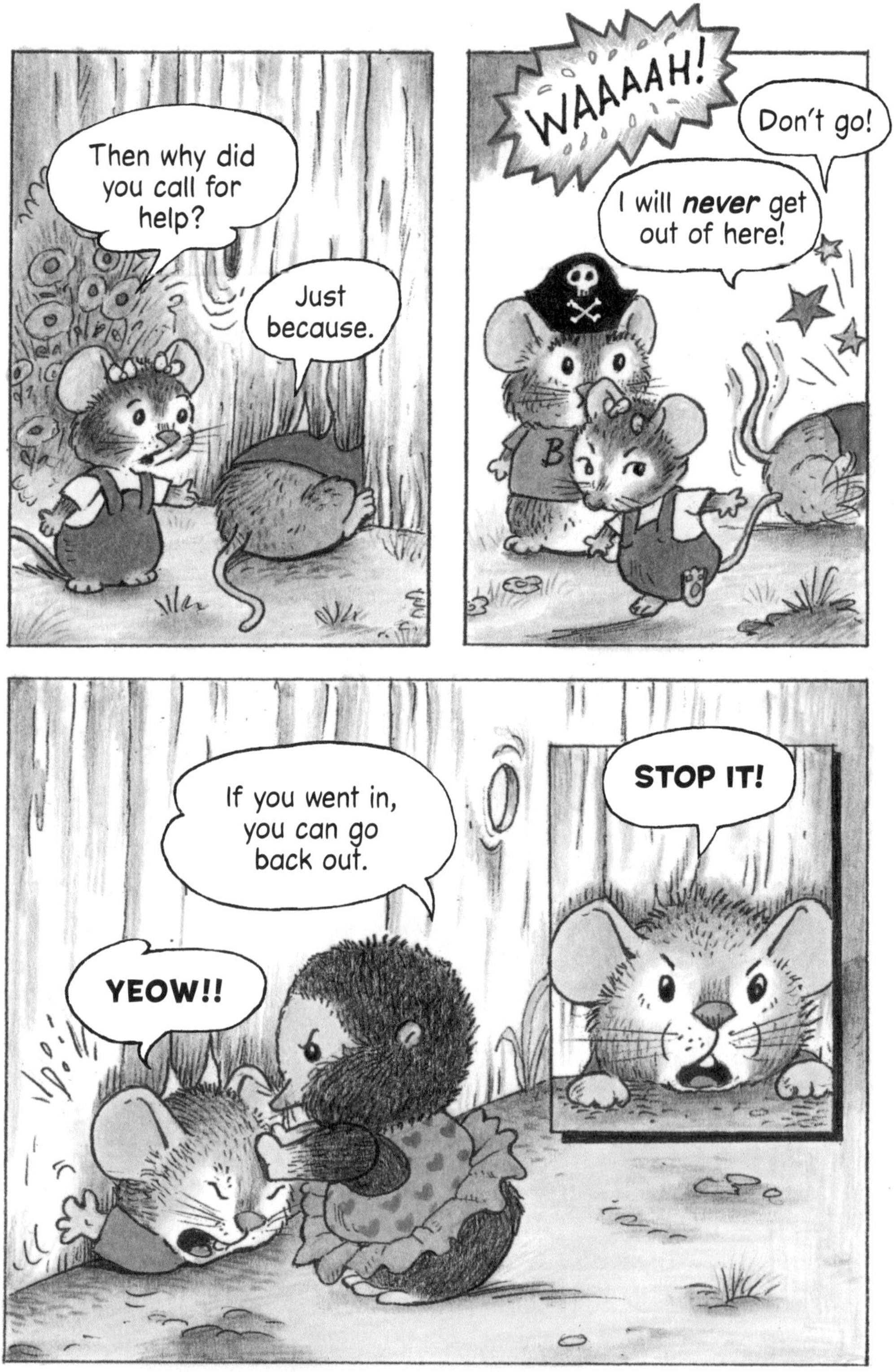
Then why did you call for help?
Just because.
WAAAAH!
Don't go!
I will ***never*** get out of here!
If you went in, you can go back out.
STOP IT!
YEOW!!

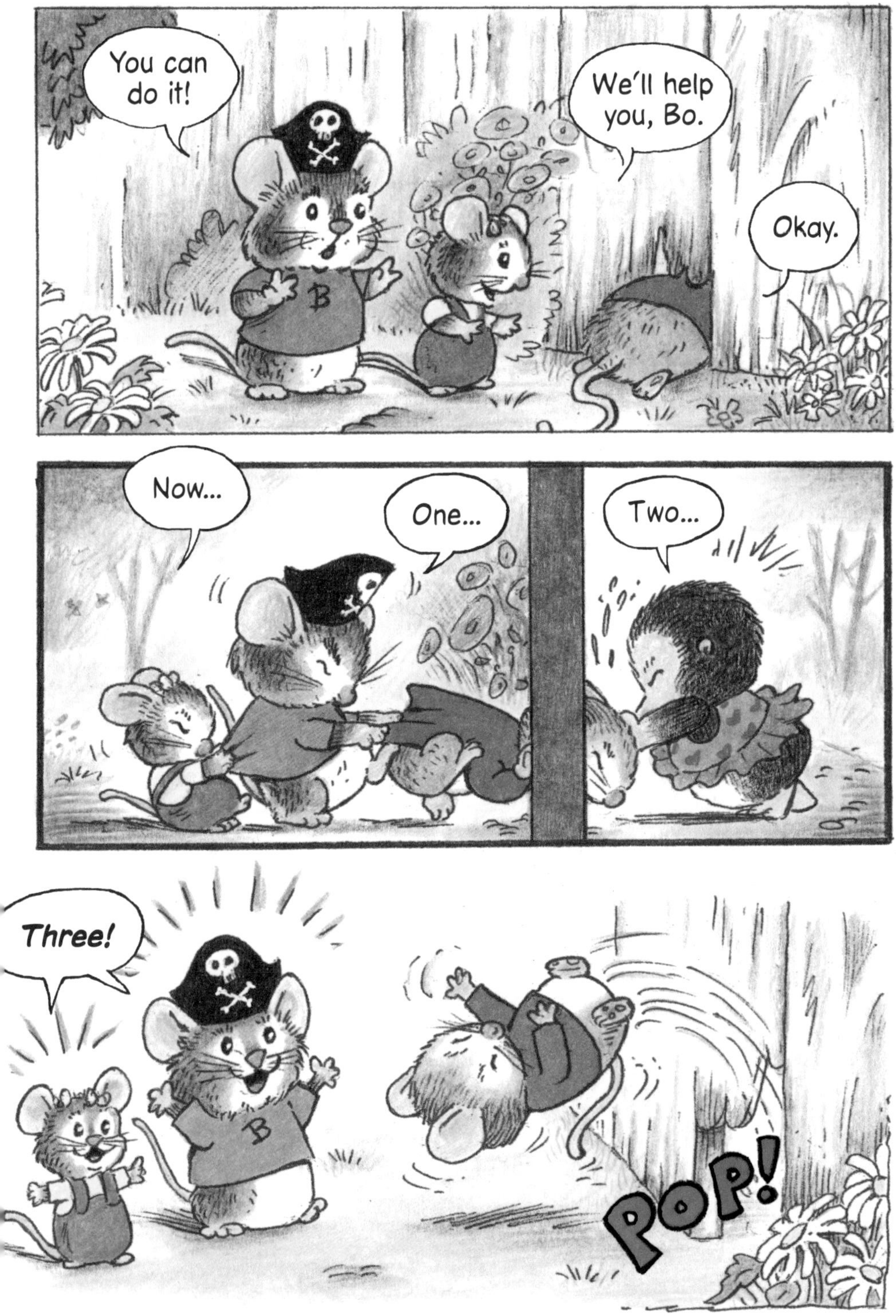
You can do it!
We'll help you, Bo.
Okay.
Now...
One...
Two...
Three!
POP!

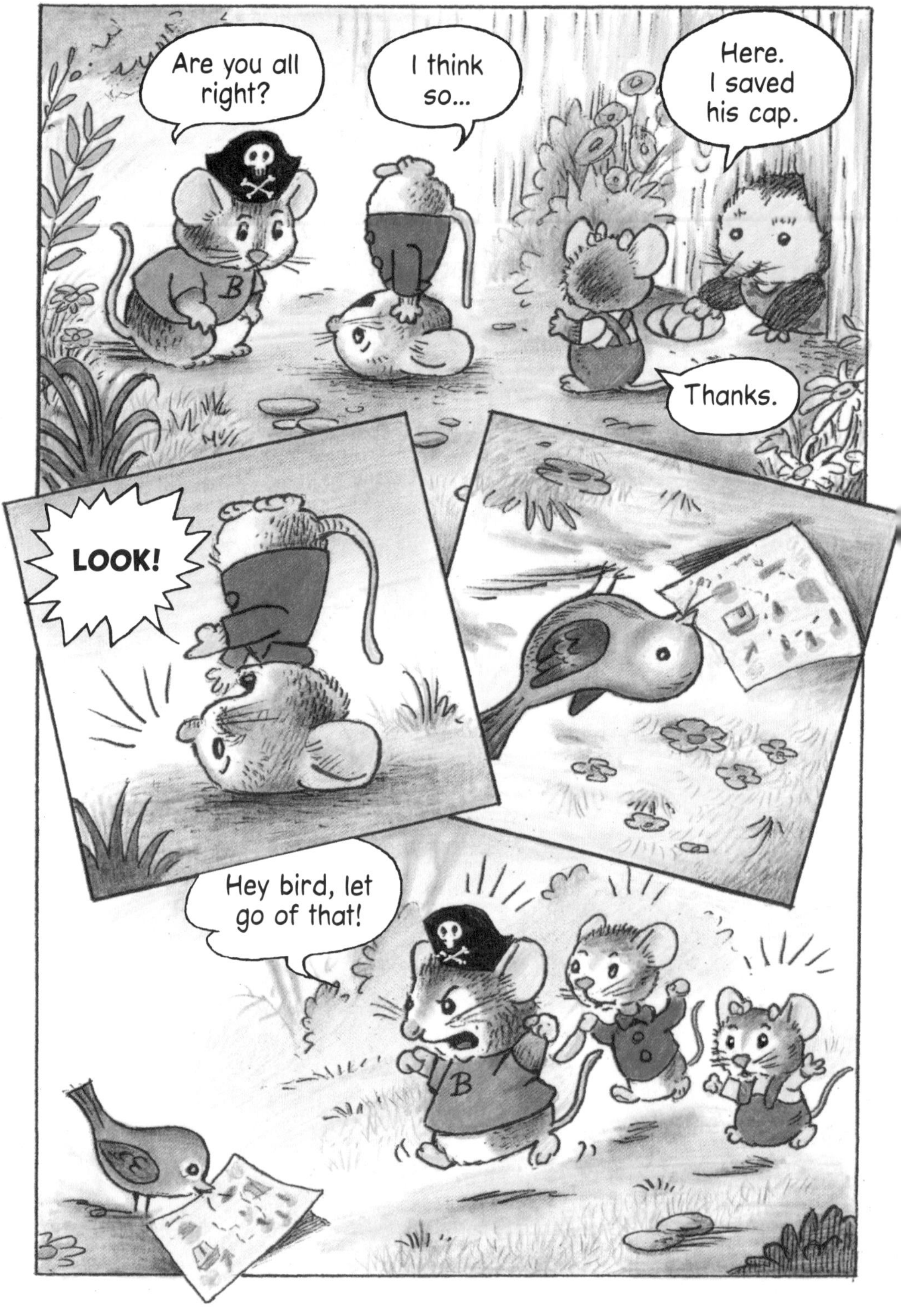
Are you all right?
I think so...
Here. I saved his cap.
Thanks.
LOOK!
Hey bird, let go of that!

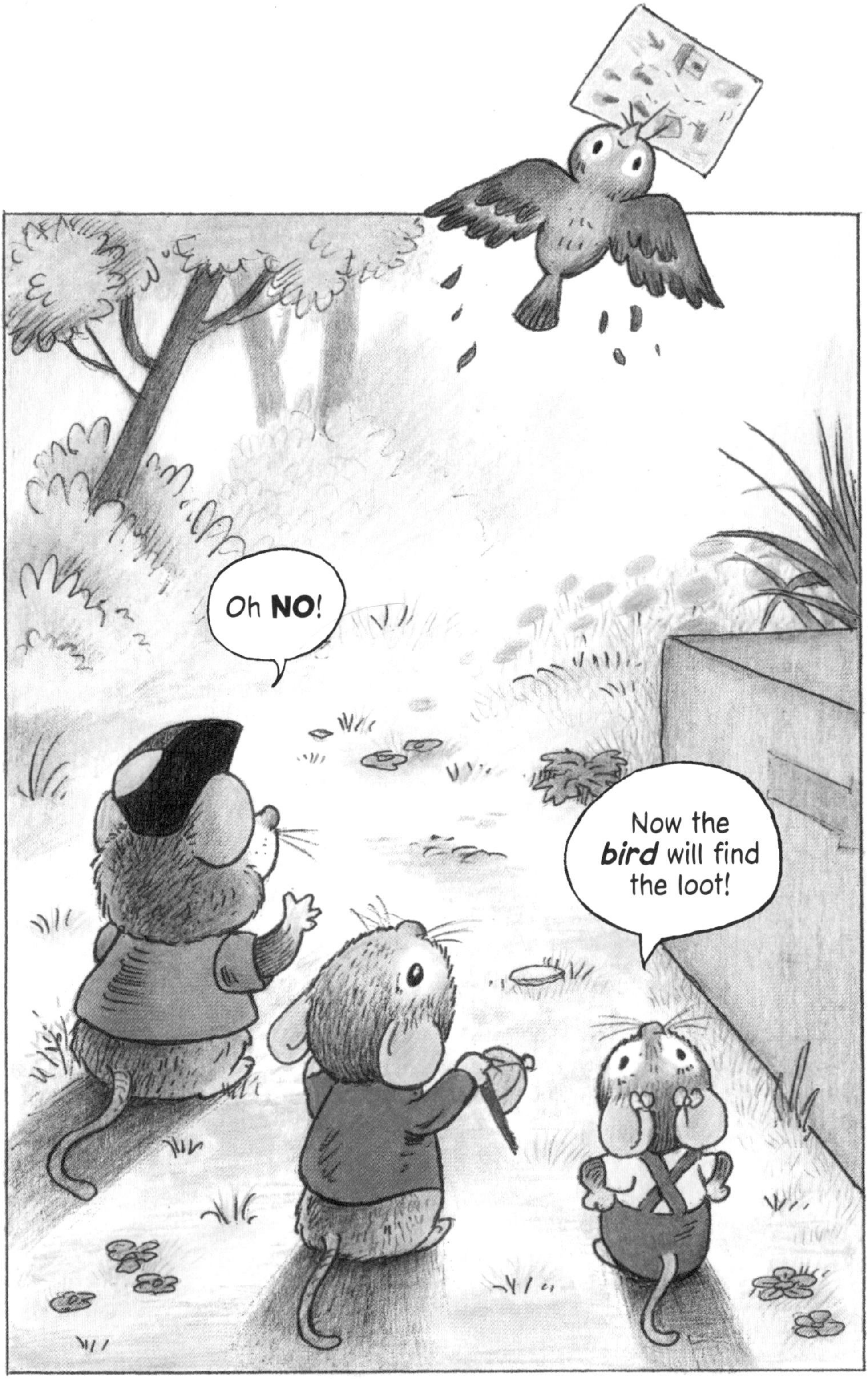
Oh **NO**!
Now the ***bird*** will find the loot!

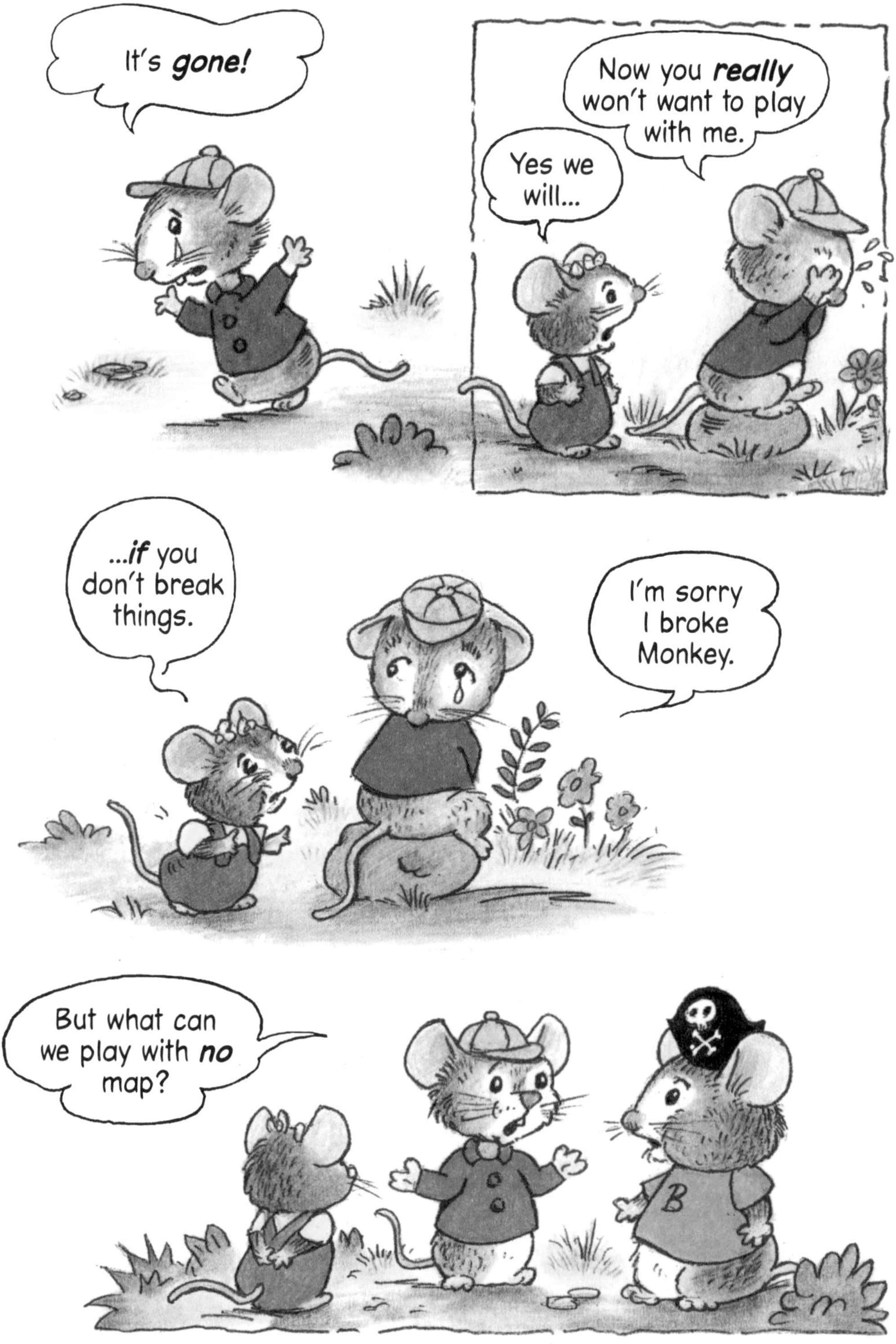
It's ***gone!***
Now you ***really*** won't want to play with me.
Yes we will...
...***if*** you don't break things.
I'm sorry I broke Monkey.
But what can we play with ***no*** map?

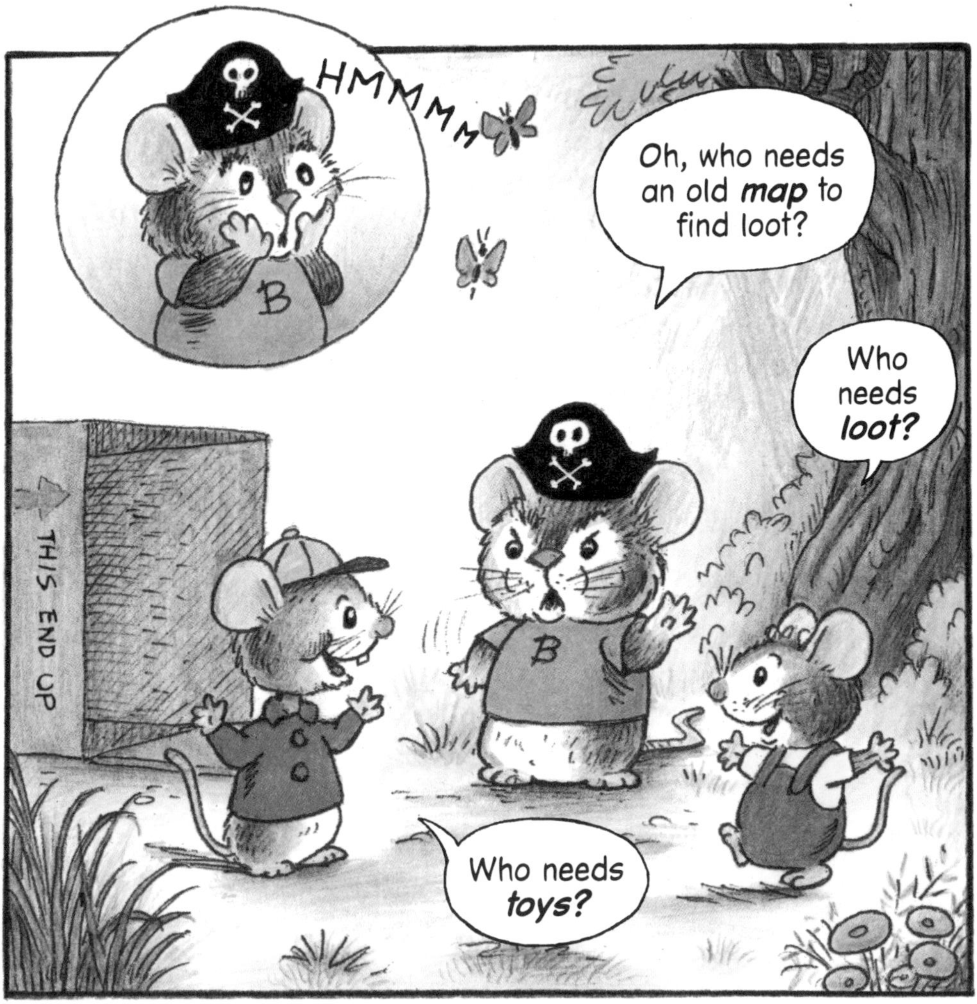
HMMMMM
Oh, who needs an old **map** to find loot?
THIS END UP
Who needs **loot?**
Who needs **toys?**

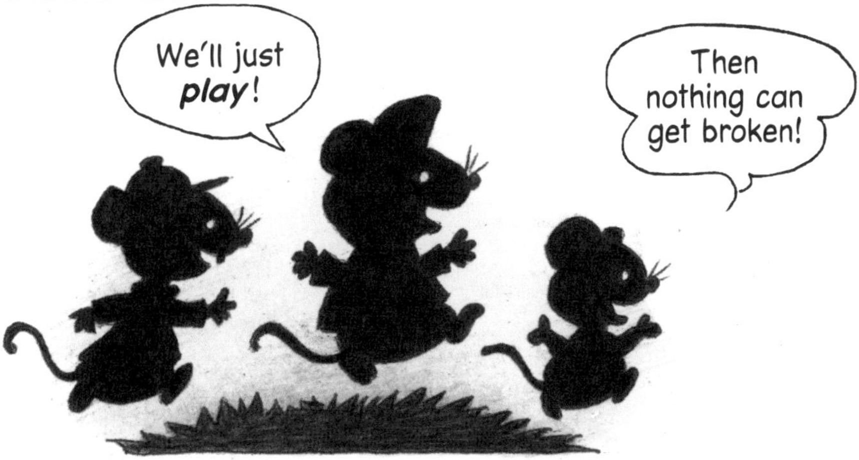
We'll just **play**!
Then nothing can get broken!

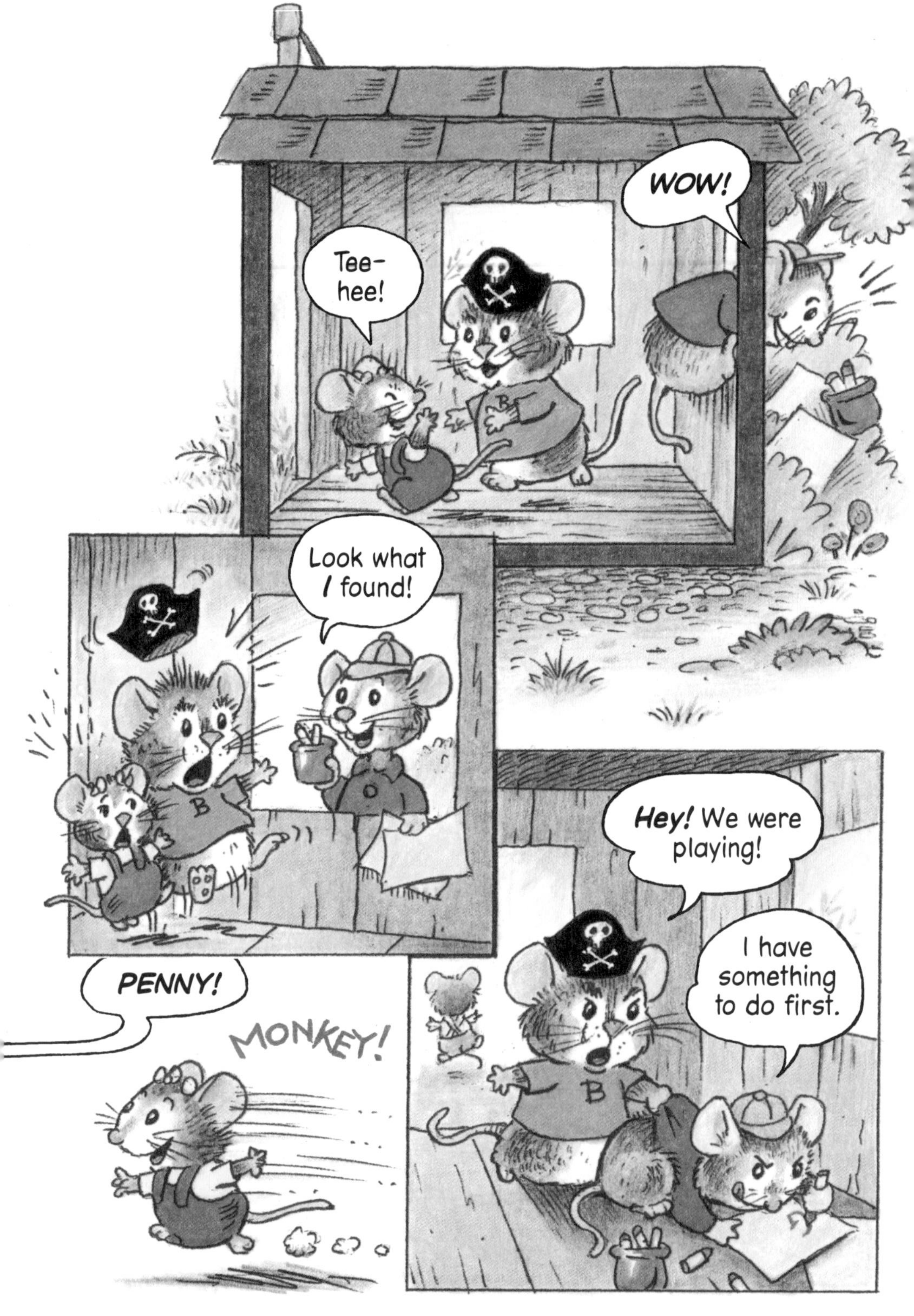
WOW!
Tee-hee!
Look what *I* found!
PENNY!
MONKEY!
Hey! We were playing!
I have something to do first.

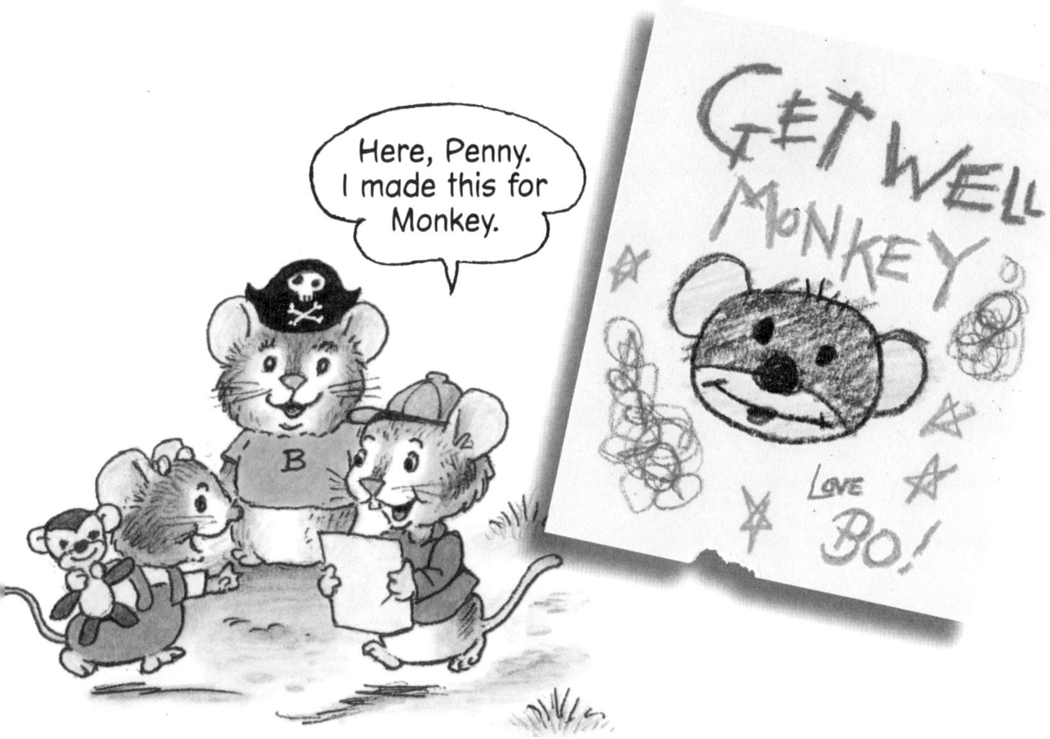
Here, Penny. I made this for Monkey.
GET WELL MONKEY
LOVE BO!

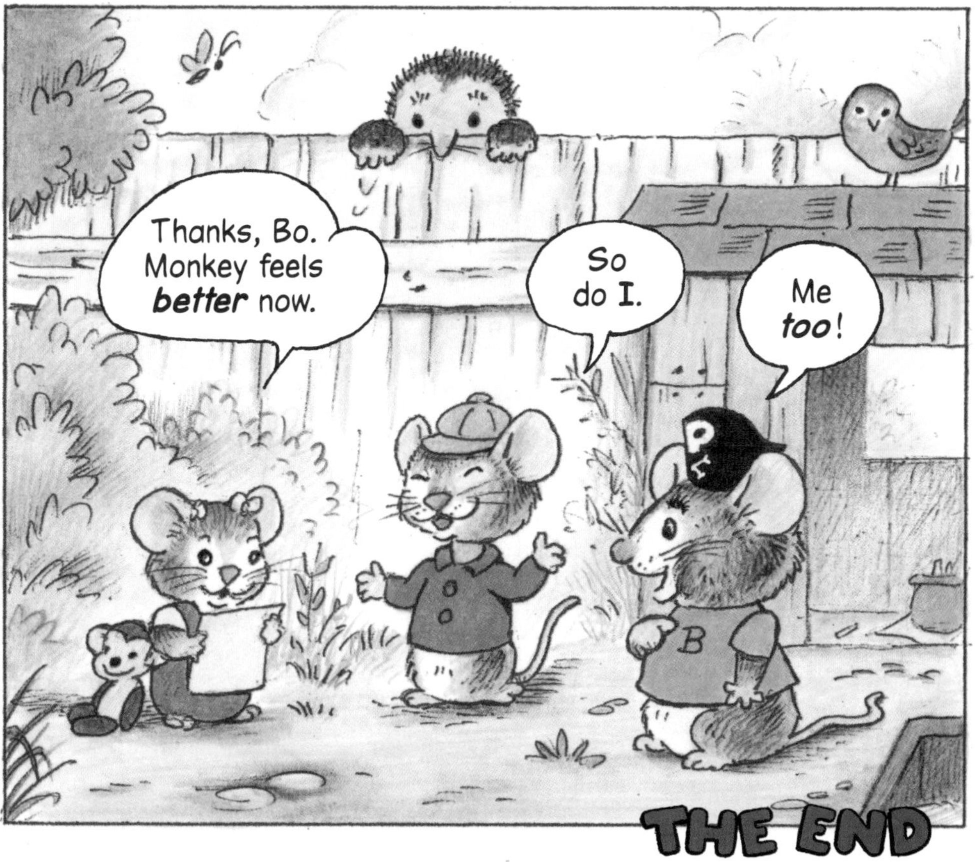
Thanks, Bo. Monkey feels *better* now.
So do I.
Me *too*!
THE END

ABOUT THE AUTHOR

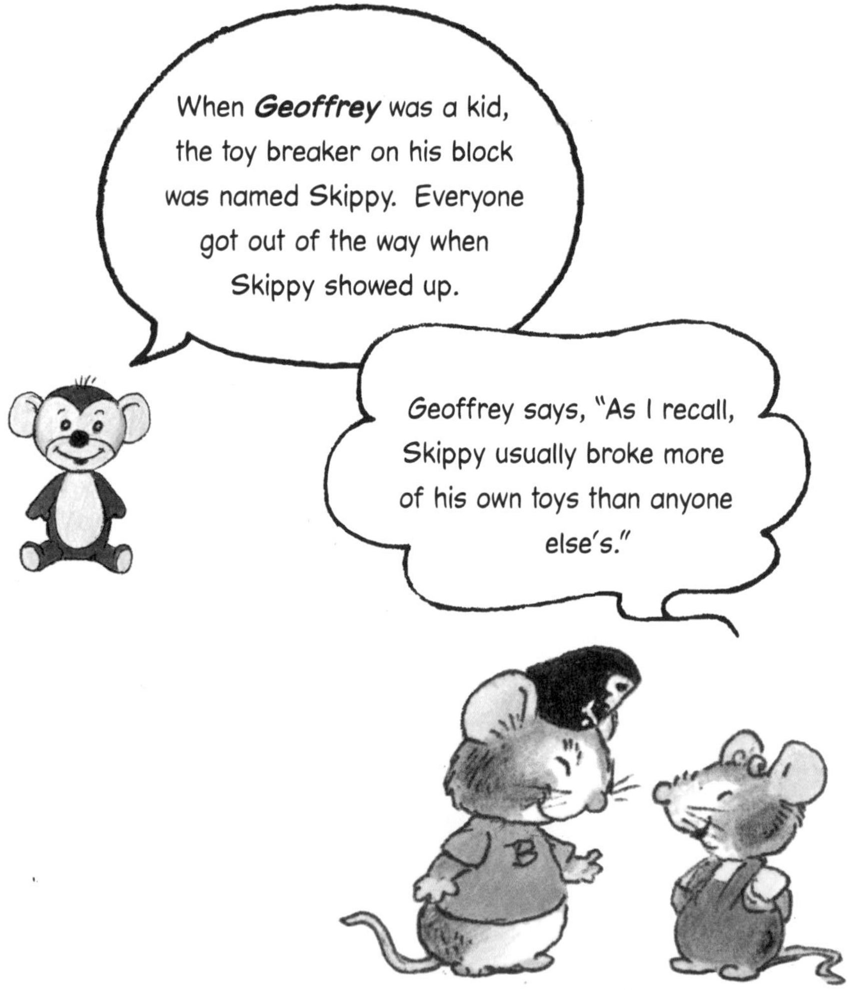
When *Geoffrey* was a kid, the toy breaker on his block was named Skippy. Everyone got out of the way when Skippy showed up.
Geoffrey says, "As I recall, Skippy usually broke more of his own toys than anyone else's."

Geoffrey Hayes has created over forty children's books, including the extremely popular series *Otto and Uncle Tooth* and the classic *Bear by Himself*. His first TOON Book, *Benny and Penny in Just Pretend*, was named a *Booklist* Top 10 Graphic Novel for Youth. In a starred review, *School Library Journal* called *Benny and Penny in The Big No-No!* a book "young children will love."

TOON INTO FUN at TOON-BOOKS.COM

TOON READERS are a revolutionary, free online tool that allows all readers to ***TOON INTO READING!***

TOON READERS: you will love hearing the authors read their books when you click the balloons. TOON READERS are also offered in Spanish, French, Russian, Chinese and other languages, a breakthrough for all readers including English Language Learners.

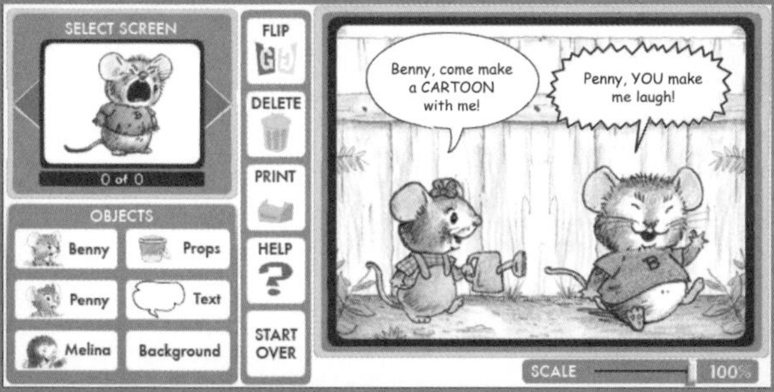

SELECT SCREEN
0 of 0
OBJECTS
Benny
Props
Penny
Text
Melina
Background
FLIP
DELETE
PRINT
HELP
START OVER
Benny, come make a CARTOON with me!
Penny, YOU make me laugh!
SCALE
100%

Young readers are young writers: our **CARTOON MAKER** lets you create your own cartoons with your favorite TOON characters.

And tune into our **KIDS' CARTOON GALLERY**: Send us your cartoons and come read your friends' cartoons. We post the funniest ones online for everyone to see!

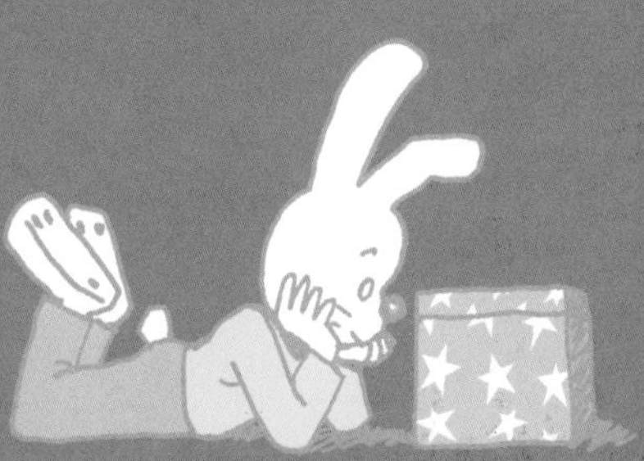